Chapter 1

Young boys dream and old ones ponder. They think about what could be ahead for them and as they get older, it's not uncommon to wonder about what might have been. That is a constant feeling that all football players have and never entirely shake. They recall the victories and defeats, but mostly they think about those games they should have won. It will always be engrained and the memories will carry over to countless discussions over endless beers 'til the end of their days.

In the playing years, in those games, so many great traits are developed: leadership, teamwork, and a razor-sharp competitive edge. However, dark habits can begin to take root. It all shapes young men into the old men they become.

* * *

It was the 1988 football season; their senior year and a great time to grow up. A time of less restriction for a teenager and long before social media and smartphones tracked your every move. They celebrated their victories and great athletic ability gave them, even more, latitude to explore life's greatest pleasures. Sure, drugs were prominent but alcohol was always king and more easily obtained. Some of them pushed the boundaries of their bodies' capabilities increasing their potential with the aid of chemical enhancement.

**UTICA EISENHOWER HIGH SCHOOL
SHELBY TOWNSHIP, MICHIGAN**

Ryan looked at his best friend, Tyler, and thought about how close they were to becoming the greatest team in school history with an undefeated season and a shot at entering the championship playoffs. The team was loaded with talent and many of them had played together for years. This, their senior year, they had dismantled every team in their path. He heard their two closest friends Jacob and Avery entering the weight room after their offense meeting.

"How was the meeting? You guys ready to go?" Ryan caught Jacob's eye.

Jacob looked confident. "Hell yes, we're going to light them up." He was a 6 foot 5 inch, 210lb quarterback with a rocket arm. The backbone of the offense, he had that All-American look with blonde hair thick as hay, square jaw, and bright blue eyes. He came from a solid athletic heritage. His father had also been a quarterback who had played for the University of Florida Gators. Full of promise and potential, sadly injuries had ended his brief career before his 20th birthday. In some ways, it seemed Jacob was to be the extension of his father's aborted career.

Avery, standing next to him, pointed at Tyler, who was getting positioned for reps on the bench press. "Just make sure you lunatics don't give up any big plays."

"Not a chance." Tyler scoffed at him.

Ryan laughed. "You guys just score some points and it's over."

Avery gave a knowing nod to Ryan. Avery was the go-to player when the team's high-flying passing attack needed some solid ground yardage. He was a tough tailback always running with something to prove. He had physically matured before everyone else. Hitting puberty in the 5th grade long before the next guy had any hair

'TIL THE END

A NOVEL OF MURDER, ADDICTION, AND LIES

By Joseph Patrick33
WITH DENNIS LOWERY

'Til the End

By Joseph Patrick33
With Dennis Lowery

"Long is the way, and hard, that out of Hell leads up to
Light."

--John Milton, Paradise Lost

The scrap torn from the newspaper sat on the table next to a three-quarter empty bottle of Crown Royal. The glass beside it had held ice—now melted—the condensation ring seeping onto a scrap of newsprint, making it translucent. A car ad bled through from the other side and the top left corner had a ragged rip where it had been torn from the newspaper:

> "...was once one of Metro Detroit's best athletes playing
> on Utica Eisenhower's first undefeated, regular season,
> football team in 1988. Services will be held July 1, 1991,
> at St. Johns Cemetery, Shelby Township."

between his legs. He had been an unstoppable force in junior high, scoring four to five touchdowns a game. It was Avery left, then Avery right... then Avery through the middle. That's all the offense the team needed. He was the Bo Jackson of middle school. As time had passed, some were able to catch up to his athletic ability, but he was still a great player and a true friend.

After five reps of 315 pounds on the bench press, Tyler dropped the last rep with a clank. "Give me a taste and a B12 pick me up and I'm good." Tyler didn't even look around, but Ryan did to make sure none of the coaches were nearby to overhear him.

Ryan slid under the bar. "Spot me," he told Tyler. He got his grip and settled himself on the bench before he started. "I understand there'll be a lot of scouts at the game."

"Yeah. I'm going to give them something to look at." Tyler grinned. At 17, he was already 6 foot 3 and 225 pounds. The only one taller than him on the team was Jacob. Tyler hoped he would stand out and catch the scout's eye at the middle linebacker position but he knew it would be difficult playing next to Ryan, who had a nose for the ball and always seemed to make big plays. Nonetheless, he was still one of the best players in school history. "What do you want on the bar? How much?" Tyler asked

Ryan reset his grip. "275."

"Pussy." Tyler grinned.

Ryan juiced but only moderately. Tyler was a demon and maybe pushed it a bit too far. But it had made him strong and very, very, quick. "How many guys have you knocked out this year, bitch?" He grinned back at his best friend.

"So did you tap Amanda yet or not?"

Ryan answered between presses. "That would be none of your business." He tried to focus on his technique. But Amanda was what most guys had wet dreams about. Every male classmate that knew her must have jerked off to her at least once. Beautiful body. Not too thin... not too thick. A luscious mouth and thick honey blonde hair that shone in the sun. Every time he saw her, he had to catch his breath. "Shit. What's the count?"

Tyler laughed. "One."

"Bullshit." Ryan gasped breathing heavily. "I think it was number five."

Chapter 2

FINAL GAME OF THE SEASON—AGAINST STERLING HEIGHTS STEVENSON BARNEY SWINEHART FOOTBALL STADIUM

Frost covered the grass as the chilly air blew the leaves from one yard to another. The morning came with the highest of expectations. They were on the verge of completing the school's first undefeated regular season. The final game, at home against their biggest rival Sterling Heights Stevenson, would determine if they remained unbeaten.

Stevenson was the team that over the years had so frequently ended Eisenhower's quest for a playoff berth. Previous Eisenhower Eagles teams had gotten to this point only to see their dreams stomped out by their biggest foe. Even when they had the superior talent, it would often come down to some poor play. It was fair to say that Stevenson had the Eagles' number.

The wet grass glistened under the stadium lights as the two bitter rivals got set to play for the league title and a spot in the playoffs. From the opening kickoff, it was clear there would be no chance of a one-play blunder to end the Eagles' season. The defense led by Ryan and Tyler stuffed Stevenson's potent offense. Tyler had three sacks and 12 tackles. Ryan had 15 tackles and one interception. Jacob was nothing short of magnificent, connecting on 23 of 28 passes for 325 yards and four touchdowns. Avery ran for a score and also caught one of the Eagles' patented, and almost unstoppable, screen passes. The night was summed up by the words of the

Stevenson coach after a 35 to 7 defeat. "We haven't been waxed like that in years."

This game gave everyone the feeling of finally getting over the big obstacle that had always kept them from greatness. A tremendous high was felt throughout the community. With this group, it was sure to carry on throughout the night; fueled by alcohol, marijuana, and cocaine. As with all the others, Ryan, Tyler, Jacob and Avery reveled in this victory. It had become expected. Their status as champions their whole life brought them certain liberties and they took advantage of them all. All the girls wanting to be by their side, a look the other way at their alcohol and drug use and forgiveness of any potential embarrassment to school or community by anyone on the team.

In the locker room, as they peeled off their drenched uniforms and tossed soiled jerseys into a bin just inside the door, an elated Coach Murphy gave the game ball to Jacob.

"Jacob, great leadership, and pinpoint accuracy tonight. I'm so proud of all of you. What can I say about the defense; you guys are the best I have ever had the privilege to coach."

Through the roars of celebration, Ryan, Tyler, Avery and Jacob grinned and turned to grab their shower bags. Each had envelopes protruding out of the vent slits of their lockers. Avery was quick to open his.

Jacob leaned over to see what it said. "What is it Avery, do the girls have something planned for us?"

"No," he grinned as he opened the note to show them all caps lettering on the single sheet of paper: CONGRATULATIONS EAGLES! YOUR PRESENCE IS REQUESTED AT THE JENNELO

HOUSE IN ONE HOUR TO CELEBRATE YOUR ACCOMPLISHMENT.

Ryan was grinning, now, too. "Nice."

"Hell yes," Jacob slapped Avery on the shoulder and flashed two high fives for Tyler and Ryan.

Avery still held the note nodding his head then looked up at his friends. "Sweet!"

They exited the showers quicker than the foamy soap off their bodies could disappear down the drain.

* * *

TYLER JENNELO'S HOUSE
SHELBY TOWNSHIP

Fifty minutes later they saw the black stretch limo parked in front of the Jennelo house when they pulled up. Tyler leaned forward in the passenger seat to look past Ryan through the driver side window at it as Ryan pulled his Chevy Monte Carlo SS in behind the yellow Trans Am in the driveway. Inside the open garage, on the left, was a black Mercedes sedan. The right side was full of boxes and a clear area for a weight bench.

"Nice ride," Jacob commented looking at it as he and Avery climbed out from the backseat of the car. They turned to Tyler, who grinned and headed to the front door. They followed him up the steps.

Tyler opened the door just as his dad was coming from his office to the left of the entry. He had overheard one of his father's phone calls the night before and suspected what was going on, but didn't know the details.

Rick Jennelo was as big as his son, only thicker-bodied with the build of a once fit man beginning to soften in middle-age. His dark hair, thinning on top, was salted with gray at the temples. "Since you told me you and your friends didn't have anything specific planned, I thought I would set up a little celebration for you. A night out at one of my friend's places downtown to celebrate your undefeated season."

Though they all lived outside the city, they knew downtown meant downtown Detroit. Mr. Jennelo's bar was on the east side but the real adult action was in the heart of the city. Ryan, Avery, and Jacob had a vague idea that Tyler's father was more than just the owner of a small bar that seemed to be very, very profitable. Tyler knew more about his dad's real business but had never been allowed to be involved or see any setting other than the bar and didn't talk to his friends about it.

Mr. Jennelo turned waving them to follow him back into his office. He sat on the corner of a large mahogany desk and faced them. "You've all turned 17 right?" They nodded. "Can I count on you to act like men—not boys—and keep something between us. And not screw up by getting too wasted and starting trouble?" He looked each of the boys in the eyes, the last and longest into Tyler's whose grin dipped and then flattened into a tight straight line. He got a "yes sir" from each of them. "Okay, then that limo is going to take you to have some fun; food, drinks, and some gambling if you want. Each of you will have a $1,000 credit limit at the tables but that's it. You reach that limit and your gambling and party is over. There will be women around..." He paused as the boys all were grinning again. "Though you can admire them and can look all you want they're not for you— no touching. Got it?" They looked at each other and he waited for their "yes sir's!" and nodded. "Okay. I've told your parents that I'm treating you to a night out on the town and they are okay with it. But don't make me regret doing this by spilling any details or acting badly." He looked at each boy. "Okay, let's go."

Outside Mr. Jennelo paused before getting in the front with the driver. "There's beer for you guys but take it easy. Okay?" He waited as they got in and heard Tyler tell Ray, the driver: "Hope you don't mind loud music while you drive." A half-second later Tyler's favorite radio station, 101.1 The WRIF, was blasting from the multiple Kenwood speakers in the passenger compartment of the stretch limo. He opened the door, slid inside and settled into the relative quiet of the soundproofed driver's area. He sensed the excitement that coursed through his son and his closest friends. Winning the game, thoughts of the next one, a playoff, and looking forward to a night of new experiences made their hearts pump. Seeing them all at this moment, so young and feeling such joy in life, touched feelings in him that he thought had been stripped away years ago. The death of his wife had taken most of what he had loved in life. Even though he still had Tyler and loved him more than he could tell him, he had been numbed by his profession's ugly side of dealing with human nature daily and could not give way easily to emotion. He regretted he had not shown more affection to Tyler as he was growing up. He glanced through the glass partition and could see the broad smile on Tyler's face and felt his own stretch his lips. This was a good thing he was doing for his son and his friends.

* * *

DOWNTOWN DETROIT

Forty minutes and six beers later, the four boys got out of the limo. The old three-story building seemed to take up a city block and looked like it needed work. It was dark without any inside lights showing. The limo had turned into an alley just wide enough to drive through. It stopped just past a set of double doors covered by a gold-striped awning. The kind that could be retracted and cinched tight against the building's wall.

Tyler's father went up the three steps to the doors and knocked four times then pressed a buzzer set to the right of the doors. At eye height—about 6 feet—a rectangular opening appeared. The light set over the doors didn't shine into it so all they saw was a white flash that blinked out as the panel slid shut again quickly.

The door opened and a big blond-haired man, taller than Jacob and more massive, greeted them.

"Mr. Jennelo..." He looked at each of the boys then back to him. "And guests... Welcome. Frank's expecting you." He backed away as they stepped into a dark, dusty, foyer. Behind the man was another set of double doors. He turned to it and pressed its buzzer. Another panel, in the right-hand door, slid open. This one was backlit by the lights inside. It shut almost as fast as it opened. Some music had leaked out along with the light and even more spilled as the doors opened wide.

"Thanks, Boris." Rick Jennelo said. He turned to Ryan, Jacob, Avery and his son. "You're at the point in life where boys become young men. Congratulations on your undefeated season." He waved them inside.

* * *

Avery looked at the pile of chips he had in front of him and jumped when someone slapped him hard on the back. He looked over his shoulder.

"Better cash those in... Ryan and Jacob shot their wad and are at the bar waiting for us." Tyler had that manic grin on his face that he wore when he was on the edge of being too high or too drunk.

Avery had seen him leave the floor an hour ago with one of the girls and had shaken his head. They weren't supposed to mess with the girls but the ones rubbing against him all night had made that hard. He made himself laugh with that thought. But the cards had been even more attractive to him. He couldn't turn away from them as the stacks of chips grew in front of him. He scooped them up and followed Tyler to the cashier. A minute later he counted the cash that was pushed across the counter back to him. Holy Shit! He'd won nearly $4,000!

At the bar, they joined Ryan and Jacob, who sat under a crystal chandelier that spun a thousand darts of light from it. The glint of the hundreds of bottles behind the long expanse of the gleaming mahogany bar was hypnotizing. Avery looked at his smiling friends and around at the opulent furnishings. He had never imagined a place like this. It felt like it was somewhere he could stay forever.

Chapter 3

TYLER JENNELO'S HOUSE

The next morning when Ryan woke up at Tyler's house, his friend's faces, and likely his, too, looked like uncooked hamburger meat left out on a plate under the sun on a hot summer day. They had polished off the remainder of a half-gallon of Crown Royal in the limo on the ride home. When it pulled into the driveway, helping each other, they stumbled inside Tyler's house to sleep off the night.

Blearily looking at each other, it was time to reset their minds and focus on their next opponent. The Sunday paper revealed the playoff matchups. The number 2 ranked Eisenhower Eagles would face the number 6 ranked Rochester team. Rochester was a team outside of the division that they knew little about, but surely they were no match for the mighty Eagles squad.

* * *

THE ROCHESTER GAME
BARNEY SWINEHART FOOTBALL STADIUM

The game was a dogfight. Almost literally. Extremely high winds had turned it into a grinding, dirty and nasty, ground war. The Utica Eisenhower Eagles aerial attack had to be shelved. Fighting the gusty wind, Jacob was just 9 of 21. It was a trench fight through three and a half quarters of both teams marching up and down the field without scoring.

Finally, Rochester's middle linebacker missed a tackle and the Eagles scored on Avery's 9-yard run late in the fourth quarter. The wind was against them for the extra point but luckily it punched through. The score was 7-0 with only four minutes left. On the kickoff, Rochester returned it to the 50. The defense dug in but Rochester was now desperate to fight their way back and ground their way to the Eagles 5-yard line with 40 seconds left.

It was first and goal. Their quarterback took the snap and handed off to the up back who hit off tackle where there was a gap to squirt through. Ryan met him in the hole, stood him up, and Tyler came in behind him and stripped the ball, recovering the fumble and sealing the victory for Utica Eisenhower.

They walked off the field winners, but it took a while to feel the urge to celebrate. The game had been far harder, far closer than they thought it would be. They had been sure they would dominate Rochester. Instead, they had barely come out with the victory and a shot to get one step closer to a state championship.

As they shook that feeling off, a tremendous sense of relief swept through the Eagles locker room. Tyler was pumped up at the win and even more so because he had a surprise to kick off their after-game celebration. They exited the locker room amidst the noise of their teammates planning their own victory celebrations. In the parking lot, in his Trans Am, Tyler passed around a double dose of mescaline. They each inserted it under their tongue on the way to the party. When they got there, it would be intertwined and mixed with their large consumption of alcohol. With an occasional toke from his favorite bong, Tyler felt the tabs of mescaline awaken all his senses.

At the party, Tyler handed a cold beer to Jacob, who was standing with Avery and Ryan in the back of the room. "If it wasn't for the wind you would have shredded them."

Jacob smiled and clapped Avery on the shoulder. "This man here got it done for us, though."

"Yeah..." They heard a voice behind them. "You guys got lucky..." The voice trailed off with a laugh.

The four of them turned to see the boy who had come in with one of their classmates, Jenny.

"What are you doing with this fucker, Jen?" Tyler's face tightened with a scowl.

"We're going out, Jennelo." Greg Stansfield answered for her.

Tyler knew who he was and ignored him. "Why'd you bring this Sterling Heights puke to our party, Jen?" He shrugged off the hand Ryan had put on his shoulder and stepped toward them.

"Please, Tyler." Jenny was worried. "We'll leave."

Greg stepped around her to face Tyler. "No, we won't."

Tyler's eyes were wide, dilated to their maximum by the mescaline. He moved closer to stand in front of him. "What do you mean we got lucky, asshole?"

In the background, the music seemed to get louder and Tyler tuned in on the song staring at Greg, the words from it in his head, 'the nature of your tragedy is chained around your neck... do you lead or are you led... are you sure that you don't care.'

Greg looked at Ryan, Jacob and Avery, who had also moved closer. "Look, you guys beat us." He nodded at Avery and rubbed his chest. "You are a hard guy to bring down." He looked back at Tyler. "But Rochester's linebacker missed that tackle in the hole. He'd been stuffing that play all game. Right?" At Avery's nod, he nodded, as well. "I'm just saying on that one play he blew it and that's all it took." He looked back at Tyler. "Your team got lucky."

Tyler bristled and tensed moving sideways from Ryan toward the middle of the room. "Leave now or I will beat your ass in front of your girlfriend." He looked at Jenny, who was white-faced, and frowned at her.

Greg moved with him away from Jenny. "Hey man, luck is part of the game." He scanned Ryan, Jacob and Avery's face. "You all know that. You played a good game and won. That's all that counts. Right?" He grinned at Tyler and held his hand out.

Tyler hit him and Greg spun backward into a table knocking drinks and bowls of chips to the floor. Red-faced he surged to his feet. Jenny grabbed his arm trying to hold him back as Ryan attempted to get between him and Tyler.

"Baby... settle down."

Tyler stopped trying to pull free from Ryan and looked around. Shelley had just come in with Amanda and two others from the cheerleader squad. She came up and hugged him. As she pressed her body against him over her shoulder, he saw Jenny leaving with Greg glaring back at him. He squeezed Shelley and heard Amanda tell Ryan. "Relax boys. Let's celebrate!"

Ryan walked over to Tyler, who was still red-faced and angry. "Are you crazy... his dad's a cop. You don't want him telling his dad and bringing the police down on you." He watched his friend closely as he cooled down. "Amanda's right..." he slapped him on the shoulder. "Let's have some fun."

Ryan and Tyler were never short of female attention. The cheerleaders particularly always had eyes for them. Amanda was Ryan's favorite and Tyler tended to her best friend, Shelley. Amanda loved to kiss, which usually went much further but she had not slept with Ryan. Shelley had done everything Tyler had asked of her. Ryan wanted a long-term relationship and was willing to wait until Amanda was ready. Tyler never really thought about tomorrow. He was all about taking pleasure in the moment and in any way that he could. Their friend Avery rotated among a handful of girls and never seemed to be pinned down to just one. Jacob was quiet and worried that the game had not enabled him to show his skills to any scouts. He wasn't really thinking about girls. He was already thinking about the next game and a closer step to a shot at what all football players dreamed of: to win a championship.

* * *

The next morning, they gathered to scout the two teams that would be playing for the right to meet them for the regional championship. They had left for downtown, nursing their hangovers with copious amounts of bottled water and Gatorade. Detroit King, the Public School League champion, was playing a smaller but well-coached and disciplined Lake Orion squad. King had superior talent with five or six Division One college prospects but their turnovers and mistakes did them in that afternoon. Lake Orion squeaked out a 24-21 victory scoring the winning touchdown on a blown coverage by the PSL champs. Orion's strong-armed quarterback found his tight-end wide open in the end zone to give them the victory.

Ryan and Jacob made small talk with the Eagles coaching staff as they exited the stadium. It was easy to see that their plan would be to shut down Lake Orion's high-powered offense by blanketing their tight-end and receivers. This would play right into the Eagles' strength. Their offense behind Jacob's rocket arm and Avery's gritty running were second fiddle to the Eagles stout defense which had yielded only 42 points the entire season. Most of those points were scored on the second team defense cleaning up in the final minutes of a blowout. Anyone who followed Utica Eisenhower football closely knew this to be their strength.

* * *

UTICA EISENHOWER EAGLES FIELD

Lucas Goldberg had graduated from Utica Eisenhower five years ago. Sitting in the bleachers, he flashbacked on when he'd been a skinny kid running around on the field that was spread out before him. He raised his camera and panned the field from left to right. At the far right, he saw the four boys as they came from the locker room and walked toward him. In the stillness of a windless afternoon, he heard the crunch and clack sound of their cleats on the track as they walked to where he sat.

He studied them. The tailback, Avery Irons, was his height but the other three were taller and seemed huge wearing full pads and carrying their helmets. They seemed so much more serious than he had been when he played here. But then he had been pretty much a scrub—second string at best—these boys were far better athletes than he'd ever been. He looked at the tallest, the quarterback Jacob Winslow, who was headed to USC; a far cry from the small college he'd gone to after high school.

"I'm glad that the coach let you take time from practice to meet with me. I'm Luke with the Detroit Times Herald. Lou Michaels is the reporter who's covered local football for 20 years but he was involved in an accident and I'm covering for him. I know that the coach and your parents heard from him about what we're doing; the profile piece on the Eisenhower Eagles undefeated season. We plan to follow you through the playoffs as far as you go. I know you're the captains of the team so let's get into it. I'll ask a couple of questions in this interview. I'd like to hear each of your thoughts and answer." He tapped the micro-recorder that sat next to him. "I'll record this and also take some notes. When we're done, I'll take a couple pictures."

The four set their helmets at their feet and leaned back against the railing, facing him, with the field behind them.

Lucas looked at the quarterback, Winslow. His stats had filled the Times Herald sports pages for the past three years during high school football season. "Lake Orion's got one of the most explosive offenses in the state. Do you think your defense can contain them?"

Winslow half turned to look at the dark-haired boy next to him. "Our defensive captains here should answer that for you. Right, Tyler and Ryan?"

He looked at the two Winslow had indicated. Tyler would be Jennelo. Michael's notes said he was the linebacker that played like a wild man. Ryan, the brown haired boy next to him, was Kramer. A sure tackler who was always in position and where he should be to defend a play. "What can you do to stop them?" he asked Jennelo.

"Knock them on their ass every time they touch the ball," he grinned at him but the smile didn't reach his eyes.

The reporter looked at Kramer. His smile was sincere. "We have the best defense in the state. We have held the teams we've played to fewer points than any other team." He nodded at Jennelo. "Our defense is gonna shut them down."

Lucas turned back to Winslow. "Lake Orion has a pretty good defense, as well."

"They do." He nodded. "But we think we can move the ball in the air or on the ground." He slapped his tailback on the right shoulder pad. Avery nodded and still looked grave, not as lighthearted as Kramer and Winslow but not as grim as Jennelo.

"And you're headed to USC. Right?" Lucas asked Winslow.

He glanced left and right at his friends then nodded with a mix of pride and embarrassment. "Yes."

The reporter focused on him because he was the one people were most interested in. "That's a big-time football program. Are you excited to showcase your talent on that stage?"

He looked at his co-captains. "My friends and I are all looking forward to what comes next in our football playing careers."

"But..." Lucas paused. "You're going to be where you stand a good shot—if things go well—to surely be seen by NFL scouts. You have the best chance of going on to play at a professional level right?"

He didn't reply and Tyler Jennelo straightened and stepped away from the railing. His shadow fell across Lucas where he sat. Jennelo looked down at him with a hard stare.

"Are we done so you can take your pictures and we can get back to practice?" He didn't wait for an answer and walked out onto the field.

* * *

That week leading up to the regional championship they were all focused and kept their noses clean. Aside from Ryan and Tyler's Thursday night ritual, it was a week of hard-hitting practice and hours of reviewing game film. The Rochester game had opened their eyes to the fact that their road to glory might be rougher than they had thought before that game.

THE LAKE ORION GAME
PORT HURON STADIUM
PORT HURON, MICHIGAN

Lucas Goldberg, Reporter Notes from The Game:

It's the day of the regional championship game, and the Eisenhower Eagles are ranked number 2 in the state and face off against the number 4 team from Lake Orion. This game is a chance for Utica Eisenhower to move into the final four for the state championship. On the long bus ride, I saw how this moment opened the door for an endless flow of emotions in these young football players. That flood converged here at the heart-pounding moment of the national anthem. I saw in their faces, and that of the coaches, that the Eagles believed their time is now. They are ready to destroy everything in their path.

The game started slowly with the Eagles offense unable to get anything going. The offensive line which was the team's only weak spot had trouble picking up Lake Orion's multiple blitz packages. The Eagles quarterback, Jacob Winslow was constantly under pressure, but the defense dominated Lake Orion's every effort when they had the ball; sacks and tackles for losses were plentiful. The half ended with a 0 to 0 score. One thing was sure; Lake Orion could not move the ball against the Eagles defense.

The second half opened with Eagles linebacker Ryan Kramer intercepting a slant pass at Lake Orion's 30-yard line. From that point the floodgates opened and the Eagles offense came to life with Jacob Winslow throwing for two touchdowns and Avery Irons running for another. The final score was 21 to 0. The Eagles football team had delivered the regional championship to Utica Eisenhower. The school that had seen so many talented players come and go, yet never had any playoff success, had arrived and its team was peaking.

* * *

After the bus ride back home, most of the team was exhausted. Though they had won, Ryan thought he and his friends should keep their celebrations to a minimum. But Tyler had different plans. He announced a victory party would take place at his house because he knew all the other players' parents would be over at Jacob's parent's house for their own party and his father would be at his bar, The Wolverine. So they fulfilled their obligation of celebration and plowed through multiple cases of beer.

Ryan spent the early part of the night comforting a troubled Amanda. Finally, he gave up. "Tyler..." he pulled his friend aside. "I'm going to take Amanda home." He glanced at her waiting for him by the front door.

"What's up with her?" Tyler grinned over at her but she didn't respond.

"Something's not right with her... she knew we'd started using at the end of the season last year. I told her we'd stopped after summer break but the other day, after the Rochester game, she found that stash of steroids in my car." He shook his head. "I'll take her home but I'll be back. Hey, we're—Jacob, Avery and me—staying over tonight, right?"

Tyler was already turning back toward the party. He smiled at Ryan, who could see how high he already was. "Sure, I called my dad and he says it's okay."

* * *

The next morning everyone was eager to pick up the newspaper and see who the Eagles would play against in the state semifinals. Mr. Jennelo had the Times Herald open and was reading it when they went downstairs.

"It looks like you're playing the number 1 ranked team, Catholic Central. They outlasted Novi from the west side of the state." He lowered the paper to look at them as they sat at the table with glasses of juice. "Those private schools..." his tone showed what he thought of them. "They have a recruiting advantage over public schools."

Ryan drank some of his orange juice. "My dad says they use that to stack their team with talent against the territorially restricted schools. He thinks they should have their own playoffs, separate from the rest of the state public schools since they have an edge in talent."

Rick Jennelo closed the paper setting it next to his coffee cup. "I agree with him. Stocked with the talent they can bring in has made Catholic Central a perennial state champion contender for years." He shook his head still clearly dissatisfied with how things were.

Ryan looked around the table at his friends and knew what they were thinking. They didn't give a shit about Catholic Central's number 1 ranking. They were always favored by the press year after year. All they knew was that Central would have to come through the Eagles and he and his teammates would be ready to fuck them up.

The Eagles still had the best, least scored upon, defense in the playoffs. Ten of the starters were seniors and this was their last shot at a championship. The only junior on the Eagle defense was a 6 foot 2 inch, 260-pound defensive tackle named Richie, who already had recruiters pounding on his door. They were bloodthirsty. It would be a great matchup for the Eagles to counter the traditional run left run right Catholic League offense. They had a very talented tailback to carry the ball behind their monstrous offensive line. Ryan and Tyler couldn't wait to get a piece of him.

* * *

UTICA EISENHOWER HIGH SCHOOL

The hype and excitement began early in the week. A wall of posters filled the hallways proclaiming the Eagles dominance. Endless encouragement from teachers or phone calls from former coaches and alumni showered the players. They were only one game away from what they believed was their destiny. A chance to get to the state championship. Players received one hall pass after another to meet with the coaching staff to review the game film for Catholic Central's tendencies.

In the Eagles weight room, they talked about it. For Ryan and Tyler, the defensive game plan was simple: nut up and stuff their ass. Offensively, they would need Jacob to create plays in space and keep them from exposing the Eagles young, undersized, offensive line. They knew that Jacob and Avery would find them some points and the defense would shut Catholic Central's vaunted offense down. Then they could start looking for turf shoes to play in the Silverdome for the championship.

After the workout that Thursday night, it was time for some player enhancement; three rails of powder and a few bong tokes between Ryan and Tyler. The next day, Friday passed as if it didn't even exist. Then it was Saturday morning and time to stake their claim to a spot to play for a state championship.

* * *

THE CATHOLIC CENTRAL GAME
ROCKET STADIUM, JOHN GLENN HIGH SCHOOL
WESTLAND, MICHIGAN

Ryan watched the weather through the locker room door. It was a cold, windy and rainy early afternoon with intermittent snow. For some unknown reason, the game was scheduled to be played on a poorly maintained high school field outside Dearborn. The neutral site was hammered by rain, eroding its surface and turning it into a sloppy track. He knew the weather would shorten their playbook and turn this game into a closed space ground pounder. When the team had arrived, the half-assed stadium was already overflowing with parents, classmates, alumni and reporters. During warm-ups on the slick turf, they had watched their oversized opponents. The players for Catholic Central were enormous.

It was just before 1:00 PM when they took the field for the kickoff. The sun peeked out for a brief moment during the national anthem. It was time. The number one and number two team in Class A for the state of Michigan were about to battle.

Lucas Goldberg, Reporter Notes from The Game:

The first play of the game, the Eagles signature screen pass to Avery Irons, went for a 68-yard touchdown. For an Eagles fan, there was no better way to start. They were up 7-0 with less than a minute into the game.

The lead only lasted for two plays. Catholic Central 90-yard returned the kickoff for a touchdown and the point after tied the score.

In the first quarter Eagles tailback, Avery Irons found success because of their over-pursuit and was able to rip off nice chunks of yardage. With the weather limiting their vertical game, it was all about yardage on the ground. The Eagles finished that drive with a 6-yard touchdown run. Catholic Central's offense was built around running the ball and they had had great success against everyone else that year. But the Eagles stiff defense, led by co-captains Ryan Kramer and Tyler Jennelo, forced punt after punt.

Late in the second quarter Eagles quarterback, Jacob Winslow, facing a stiff wind, threw an interception in their own territory which Catholic Central capitalized on off the foot of their All-State kicker with a 40-yard field goal to end the half. The Eagles were still up 14-10.

The second half began just like the first with the Eagles defense forcing three and outs. Their offense struggled to move the ball on the ground and through the air with the gusting wind. It became a game of trading punts. After another failed drive by Catholic Central, the Eagles took over on their 40-yard line. Two runs by Avery Irons and an incompletion by Jacob Winslow left them facing a third and six. After a failed try to draw them offsides, they were faced with a fourth and 11 attempt at their 49-yard line. For some unknown reason, the Eagles coaching staff decided to go for it. The quarterback, Jacob Winslow dropped back to pass, eluded three defenders and scrambled to the right side of the field. He fired a strike downfield that was caught, but by the wrong team. It was right into the hands of a Catholic Central defensive back at their 40-yard line. [To this day the call is still scrutinized especially after the Eagles punter's great performance. It was later divulged that the coaches were worried because of some close calls when the Eagles line broke down resulting in some nearly blocked punts.]

Catholic Central quickly took the field to capitalize on Utica Eisenhower's mistake. Their first two plays were stuffed by the stingy Eagles defense as Catholic Central leaned on their weary tailback to make the play and keep the clock running. On third and 11 typically conservative Catholic Central pulled out possibly their only trick play; a halfback pass. Their battered tailback ran wide and threw up a duck which was deflected only to hit the helmet of the Eagles strong safety and bounce into the hands of their big tight-end who fell into the end zone for a touchdown. It was the ugliest of plays that can't be explained other than it was just a fluke.

Down 17-14 with only two minutes and six seconds left on the clock Eagles quarterback, Jacob Winslow now had to bring them back and take it down the field and win the game for Utica Eisenhower. The ensuing kickoff was out of the end zone by Catholic Central's soon to be Michigan Wolverine kicker.

The Eagles offense took the field. They had to be the ones to pull them out of an impending disaster. On the first play, Jacob Winslow found Avery Irons on a halfback wheel route for a 30-yard pickup. The next two plays were two quick passes, lasers, by Winslow to get them down to the Catholic Central 11-yard line with 45 seconds on the clock. The Eagles had one timeout left. The coaching staff gathered on the sideline to determine what shots to take at the end zone that would best manage the time remaining on the clock. The play was sent in.

Jacob Winslow dropped back to pass and it was a seeming perfect play call with all the pressure coming from the outside. Winslow deftly brought the ball down and handed off to the tailback, Avery Irons, on an inside draw. Irons slid past the first defender into an open space down to the 5-yard line. There he was hit by Catholic Central's middle linebacker hard enough to jar the ball loose. It bounced once, spun, then settled. The ball seemed to sit there on the grass for a lifetime until a Catholic Central defensive back covered the football.

Game over and Catholic Central moves on to the championship game.

* * *

Ryan and Tyler looked on from the sidelines. There it was. Their football life lying there on the 5-yard line. As their opponents stormed the field to celebrate, they realized they had lost the game that they all had worked together for 10 years to win. They had come into it sure that they would. But it was over. It was all over.

Chapter 4

**AVERY IRONS HOUSE
SHELBY TOWNSHIP**

The clock radio showed 3:10 PM. "And with that fumble recovery Catholic Central can run out the clock. It's game over for Utica Eisenhower's Eagles and the end of their perfect season. Catholic Central moves on to the state championship..."

The elderly woman turned off the radio and thought of her boy—her grandson—that had been the one to lose the football. She remembered what she had told his father when he'd given him his first football on his eighth birthday: "He's going to get hurt playing that game. It's bound to happen. Even young bodies can break with all that tackling and hitting... All that hurting each other." For many young boys and young men, she knew that sports were their only hope. But still she worried about her boy. He was all she had after his father had died and left him in her care. But 10 years on he had grown up carrying that ball with him everywhere. When he was younger, she even had to slip it from his sleeping arms and put away at night only to have him pick it up again first thing the next morning. Over those 10 years, he also had grown up faster and stronger than his friends and when this last year so many of them caught up with him it made him try to hold onto his dreams even harder. She remembered all the times he had told her:

"Grandma, I'm going to take care of you and you can go on one of those Holy Land cruises you keep those magazine articles and advertising on. You'll see... I'm gonna do it for you. I love you, grandma."

This past year, though harder on the field, had been magical for him and his friends to go unbeaten and get into the playoffs. She had heard the excitement in his voice and seen the light in his eyes when he was around his friends talking about it after each game, with each victory. She was so very proud of him. But he was so sure football would deliver to him all that he wanted that he didn't focus on his school work and she couldn't get him to change that. And now in one of the most important games he'd ever played she knew he was going to blame himself for fumbling and losing it for his teammates. She had known he would get hurt playing football and knew how he was feeling right now. Pride hurts most when it falls as hard as it had today for her boy. She hoped she could help him shake it off, not dwell on what had happened, and focus on his future. She had set aside enough money to get him through college and give him a start in life that no one in her family had ever had.

* * *

ROCKET STADIUM, JOHN GLENN HIGH SCHOOL

Standing there watching another team celebrate in front of us was heart wrenching. Trying to hold back all the emotions was impossible. I looked at Tyler, who turned to me with a wild look on his face.

"Ryan, what the fuck just happened?!"

We were blindsided by a loss we never expected and the floodgates were opened. The pain was felt throughout the entire silver and blue. Outplaying and outgaining our opponent 305 yards to 92 yards didn't matter. All that mattered, all that would be recorded forever, was the final score. A 17-14 loss.

Our numb bodies exited the stadium, dragging an inconsolable Avery with us. We were done, eliminated, and nothing could be said to change that reality. I'll never erase that image of Avery clawing for the ball as if his life depended on it. In hindsight, maybe it did. I'll never forget the devastated look on his face when the offense came off the field.

It took 45 minutes into the long bus ride to even budge Avery out of his dark descent. Back at school in our locker room, we banded together in uniform for one last time. We had no reason to celebrate but decided to stick with our plan and go to Torch Lake. We separated to go home and grab some things. After quick assurances to my parents that everything was fine, I waited for Tyler and Jacob to pick me up in Tyler's Trans Am. Thirty minutes later I saw him pull in. "Mom, Dad... they're here. I'm going." Grabbing my bag, I didn't wait to hear them tell me to be careful. I needed to get going and put this day behind me.

I climbed in and was as silent as my friends as we made our way to get Avery. The sky was filled with sleet pelting Tyler's windshield. The ice added to our numbness but inside each of us was beginning to burn our anger at the loss.

AVERY'S HOUSE

The three entered Avery's house to be greeted by his concerned grandmother. Sick with the flu, she hadn't gone to the game and had listened to it on the radio. They could tell by her look when she opened the door that she had known what to expect when her grandson got home. But it had been worse than that.

"He's a mess. I'm glad you boys are here. Maybe you can get him to stop blaming himself."

They went upstairs to find Avery lying on his bedroom floor staring at the ceiling and listening to his Walkman. Through his headphones they could hear INXS singing, *Never Tear Us Apart.*

"Avery," Tyler said. He didn't respond. "Avery!" Tyler was louder.

Jacob took a step forward and dogpiled Avery to get a response. He started to struggle underneath him and Ryan couldn't help but laugh at the sight. "Get up. Let's go motherfucker. We're going up north to flip the switch on this shitty day."

Jacob got up on his knees but Avery still laid there with his eyes closed. Tyler walked over and poked him in the ribs with his foot. "Some of Shelley and Amanda's friends are coming…" He looked around to make sure Avery's grandmother wasn't nearby. "You know that cute chick, Brenda with the big tits and the short blonde hair." Tyler's grin spread across his face and he poked Avery in the ribs again. "Come on man. You know you want some of that and Shelley says that she said she thought you were hot."

Avery sat up. "Okay—okay, let me throw some stuff together." He walked over to his dresser and started pulling clothes out.

"I knew it." Tyler laughed. "Big tits and blonde hair that'll get you going every time."

But Avery didn't smile and didn't comment. He put the clothing in a bag and turned to face his friends. "Let's go." In the hallway he turned into the bathroom and grabbed shampoo and cologne, unzipping his bag he tossed them in and headed downstairs. They followed him and at the foot of the stairs Avery's grandmother pulled Jacob aside. She knew the boys celebrated their wins but worried what would happen with how they dealt with a loss.

"Don't you let him drink—he's not in a good way." She was a tiny lady and seemed even smaller looking up at Jacob.

He nodded. "Don't worry ma'am I'll keep an eye on him and stay at his side while we're up there and make sure nothing stupid happens."

"Good." She reached a thin hand up and patted him on the shoulder. "That's what real friends do for each other."

They packed themselves into Tyler's Trans Am, not an easy thing given their size, and 10 minutes later they stopped to pick up some roadies before jumping onto I-75. Tyler went into the party store and used his age-appropriate ID card that the four had crafted for each of them on the south side of Detroit. He came out with two cases of Labatt's and a half-gallon of Crown Royal. The other party favors were packed away in his golf bag; too risky to be used on the four-hour drive to Torch Lake.

Nonstop music from Metallica, AC/DC and Guns & Roses rang in their ears for the whole drive. It served an unintended purpose as it limited the possibility of a discussion about what the hell had happened at the game. The only outburst about it was surprisingly from Jacob as Tyler changed the music.

Being the tallest, he rode shotgun because he needed the legroom. Suddenly, he slammed his fist on the dashboard; its plastic popped and shook.

"Hey watch that shit man!" Tyler took his right hand off the steering wheel and backhanded Jacob on the shoulder. "What's your problem?" his eyes went back to the road. The sleet was now mixed with large flakes of snow that slanted down through increasingly gray clouds.

Jacob half turned in the seat so he could see Ryan and Avery, too. "How could they have scheduled the game—a fucking playoff game—on that sorry excuse of a field?" He shook his head. "And we were stuck running the fucking ball most of the time." He didn't mean for his eyes to stop and focus on Avery.

Ryan felt Avery stiffen next to him in the small back seat of the Trans Am. He looked at Jacob, who had turned back around to face the windshield. They all realized their rage and frustration needed to be contained. Because if Avery felt they were blaming him, he would have a meltdown to end all meltdowns. He looked at the back of Tyler's head and stole another sideways glance at Avery. He couldn't help but think bottling it up was just putting off dealing with how each of them felt. And he suspected that wasn't a good thing but he kept his mouth shut. Later, at some point at the lake, they would get it all off their chest.

They exited I-75 at Grayling on Highway 72 West to head northwest toward Tyler's father's cabin just southeast of Eastport. They stopped again at a convenience store to grab more booze and wine coolers for their female guests. When they went in, they heard the weather announcement on the radio: "By the end of the weekend looks like we will have six or seven inches of snow on the ground in the lake area." In ten minutes they were back on the road.

* * *

TORCH LAKE 10:30 PM
THE JENNELO'S LAKE CABIN

Fifty-one miles west and north later they were pulling up to Mr. Jennelo's lake cabin at the northern tip of Torch Lake. As they slowed to a stop, they saw other cars and trucks parked in front and on one side of the cabin. Behind the cabin, they saw the glow of a large bonfire. Snow was still falling and there was already two fresh inches on top of the six inches already covering the ground.

Tyler got out and stretched. They were all stiff from the long ride and more than a little sore from the game. "Looks like some of our classmates got here ahead of us." Tyler grinned at Ryan as he got out of the car. "Good thing I gave Eddie a heads up to have things ready."

Leaving everything in the car, they walked around to the back. Ryan saw that Amanda was there with five of her friends. A month after the school year had started, they had patched things from a break up over an argument that summer. Things had been kind of tentative between them since but when she saw him she quickly rushed to hug him. Soon they were surrounded by sympathetic friends.

Eddie, one of their friends who had graduated the year before and whose father also owned a cabin nearby, came up to Tyler. "Man, unseasonable weather we're having even for up north..." He did it in his best Mr. Potter 10th grade science teacher's voice. "Hey," he said in his normal voice. "Like you asked, I got things ready for you." He waved a gloved hand at the bonfire. "I went ahead and wheeled out your two new snowmobiles and checked them... and that older one, the third, I got it to fire up and it's sitting over there next to the others—you need to check its tank, though. The gauge doesn't work." He motioned over to the left of the bonfire close to the door of the cabin. The snowmobiles were pointed toward an open field that now had an even blanket of fresh, crisp snow on it gleaming under the moon. "With the fresh snow, there should be some fun in the field and on the trails around the lake." He looked over at the girls next to them. "Assuming you have any time for that, I mean." He grinned and tipped his cap at Ryan as he went over to warm his hands by the fire.

In no time the music was playing loud, the grill was stuffed with filets and the booze was flowing. Eddie was in charge of the grilling and he cooked the meat to perfection while Jacob made a jungle punch consisting of seven different bottles of booze mixed with several flavors of fruit juice. Tyler got out a shallow rectangular pan from the kitchen and sorted out rails of powder and the party was in full swing. Avery was quiet but he partook in everything that was available.

Tyler walked over to Ryan, offering the pan full of white lines, and commented. "The record will go down tonight. Follow me guys." He was making a reference to his father's breathalyzer that was given to him by his longtime friend Mike the state trooper. Tyler's father didn't know it but he kept a log book on the highest reading taken during their frequent binges at the cabin during the summer. Jacob held the title with an impressive .32 reading after finishing off a bottle of tequila and not leaving the worm behind. As a result, they didn't hear from him for a few days after their Fourth of July three-day bender. He took the idea from the movie Urban Cowboy, claiming he would have visions of the future. He never gave much insight into those visions during his two-day bout of dry heaves. He only vowed that he would never do it again.

Inside, Tyler took the breathalyzer out of a drawer and tested his blood alcohol level to be .19, Avery was .17, Jacob was .16 and Ryan also at .16. All were clearly over the legal limit, but with their experience they had plenty of room to run. The girls had followed them in and soon Avery looked more comfortable on the upper level and intimate with Brenda.

Ryan looked around the cabin and found she had come inside with a couple of her friends. The only girl he had ever loved, Amanda; an unassuming yet beautiful girl who satisfied him in every way. Blonde hair, striking blue eyes with unblemished C- cup breasts. She always made him feel good and had a calming effect. One thing was for sure, she knew him better than anybody literally inside and out. Their only problem was his intermittent temper which caused short-term breakups. They each wanted to maintain a serious relationship but it was hard. Ryan knew this for certain. He loved her simply because he would never grow tired of kissing her sweet lips. He had thought about her a lot on the drive from Shelby. Losing that football game hurt and she had always been there to help him through dark times. She was also the one that kept him focused on using his natural intelligence and one of the reasons why even with the dedication to football and working out he had the third highest GPA in the class. That was why he had received three scholarship offers from Ivy League schools, including his father's alma mater Cornell University.

He worried about that; going off to Ithaca, New York for four years. Amanda was smart too, and could get into any number of colleges but she was stuck. Her mother needed her here to work and help pay for her father's medical care. He shook his head. It was a fucked up situation and he hated to leave her behind. But even if she could go with him, his studies and playing football wouldn't leave him much time for a relationship. And it had to be even harder for a long distance one to make it. But he couldn't pass up playing football at his father's college. That was something his father had dreamed of since he was born. His father's vision was for him to get his four-year business degree with an MBA to follow. He felt that was the foundation for long-term success in life and it had proved the correct one for him.

He walked over to where Amanda was talking to Shelley, who was clinging to Tyler. She smiled at him as he stopped beside her and leaned down to whisper, loudly, in her ear. "Let's go sit by the fire and leave these two... to whatever." Ryan rolled his eyes and smiled. Tyler grinned back and tugged Shelley toward his bedroom.

Outside there was still a group of people clustered around the fire. No one was sitting on the large log that had been rolled up facing it. Ryan led her to it and sat down. "Amanda, I'm sorry about how things have been... About how I've been since the summer. I'm glad you came up here so we could be together."

She hugged his arm and slid closer to him. "I know how you are. How you feel about things, especially going into this football season. But it's paid off. You got a scholarship to Cornell and that's one of the best schools in the Ivy League. You should be very proud. Losing that game today doesn't really mean anything when you think of what's ahead for us. But we have to talk about what's going on with you... that's been affecting us."

He didn't know how to tell her how he felt—about the game and the hardest thing, for him—about her. He knew he loved her and didn't want to screw things up any more than he had already. He didn't know if she would give him another chance if he did. "Amanda, I—"

Chapter 5

**TORCH LAKE
THE JENNELO'S LAKE CABIN**

"Ryan!"

He looked around at the shout out to him then ignored it and turned back to Amanda. "I'm fine. Just losing that game... that's fucked up."

She could see the cords standing out on his neck. A sure sign he was holding his temper in check. "Ryan, it's not just the game. You're angry—on edge—all the time. You've been that way all year. Ever since you started using those-"

"Hey, Ryan!" The voice was louder. Eddie stepped through a circle of people around the bonfire to the log where Ryan and Amanda sat.

Ryan looked at Amanda, now glad for the interruption. "What's up Eddie?" He stood and was a full head taller than him. Eddie's normal grin was gone. He looked serious. Glancing at Amanda, he gave a little sideways tilt of his head and stepped away. Ryan followed him a few feet from the fire and looked down at Eddie. "Okay, what's up?"

"There's a girl looking for you. She said her name was Kelly." Eddie scanned around them his eyes pausing on Amanda, who had remained on the log but was watching them. "She's pretty messed up."

There was a commotion in the group of people behind them. They both heard her now. "Ryan—Ryan Kramer!" She was coming closer.

"Shit! That's her." Eddie looked to Ryan's right as a thin dark-haired girl pushed between two people shoving them to either side. She was breathing heavily. The light from the fire wasn't what caused the shadows under her eyes. Her pale face was drawn above the padded parka that didn't hide her thinness.

She saw Ryan and headed straight for him. "I need to talk to you." She looked at Eddie and over at Amanda. "Alone," she emphasized and hugged her arms tight around her chest trying not to shake.

Fuck, Ryan thought. "Let's go inside." He gestured at the door into the cabin if you could call a 4,000 square foot building a cabin. As he took her inside, he saw the look Amanda gave him. He shook his head; I'll deal with that later. He shut the door behind them putting his back against it to block the glass from any curious eyes.

Still shaking, she glared up at him. "I'm pregnant."

"Christ, Kelly," he swore. "It was just a couple of times are you sure it's me?"

Her voice pitched higher and louder. "I need money."

"For what? An abortion?" He looked at her and could tell she was hurting bad but it didn't have anything to do with being pregnant. "Or do you really need it for more drugs?"

"I'm gonna tell." The wild look in her eyes convinced him she would. "Your parents. Everyone." She walked to the side table and brushed her fingers across the phone. He moved closer to her to snatch the phone away in case she picked it up and started dialing "I don't have any money."

"You football gods can find money somewhere." She looked around at the expensive furnishings in a house used only part-time for holidays and vacations. It was almost four times the size of the rickety-walled tract home she'd grown up in with her sister, brother, and parents. "Maybe your friend Tyler can get it from his rich dad. He loves you jocks."

They both heard someone coming out of one of the rooms. "She thinks she can squeeze money out of you?" It was Tyler, shirtless, pulling his pants on. From the room he had left they heard a girl's laugh. He looked behind Ryan. "Oh! Hi, Amanda." He said awkwardly.

"What's going on?" Ryan turned and Amanda was just inside the front door.

Kelly pushed past Ryan and walked up to her. "Ask," she sneered, "your football hero boyfriend." She stepped around Amanda and opened the door, looking up at the elaborate lighting suspended from the high ceiling over the entry. She shook her head and paused for a last shot. "I'll talk to you later, Ryan." She looked from him to Tyler. "You guys got it knocked... everything you want. But at some point, you'll pay." With a final stabbing glare at Ryan she left with, "You can bet on that."

Chapter 6

**TORCH LAKE
THE JENNELO'S LAKE CABIN**

"What was that about?" Amanda asked Ryan ignoring Tyler, who now seemed focused on zipping and buttoning his blue jeans.

"She's not anyone to worry about," Ryan said moving to shut the door.

Amanda was usually a quiet girl but she had the kind of still waters that run deep. "I know who she is—the whole town does—and it sounds like you do have something to worry about."

"Amanda, it's nothing."

"You say that about a lot of things Ryan." She noticed Tyler sidestepping toward the bedroom he'd come out of. "You too, Tyler and you both know what I'm talking about."

A girl's giggle and call came from the bedroom. "Tyler, you coming back?" Amanda walked past Tyler to look inside. "Hey there Amanda," the voice asked. "You want to party, too?"

She whirled on Tyler, who had followed her. She pushed him on the chest. "You got Shelley high?"

"Amanda?" She turned and Shelley was in the doorway; a sheet she had wrapped around her slipped baring her breasts. She looked back at Tyler, who was staring at Shelley's chest and grinning. She pushed him again and glared at Ryan.

"You're both fucking assholes!" She stormed out slamming the front door behind her making the glass shake.

"You better go after her." Tyler had retrieved his shirt and shoes. He looked up from tying the laces of his boots. Just as he stood, the door burst in, shattering the stained glass picture of the sun setting over the lake that was inset in the door. The man who stepped in wasn't as tall as either of them but his powerful, stocky build had the thickness of a mature man. He looked at Tyler. "I know you…" He turned. "And you must be Ryan, then." He moved toward him.

"Gavin, wait." Tyler stepped in front of him. "Don't-" the man hit him hard. The blow to the face spun him to one side.

Gavin launched himself at Ryan, getting him by the throat and driving him into a wall and shattering the mirror over the wet bar. "I followed Kelly, motherfucker. You're the one that knocked her up!"

"Get off him you fuck." Tyler yanked him off of Ryan.

Gavin wheeled around and kicked him in the balls, then charged after Ryan again who was back on his feet.

"What the hell is going on?" Avery elbowed his way through the cluster of gawking classmates at the door.

Gavin kicked Tyler in the face and shoved Avery as he tried to grab him. He backed toward the door. "I'll find you when you're not with your friends, fucker." He rushed outside.

Tyler was up from the floor but bent over holding his face. His nose, broken and bleeding, was already swelling. He straightened and Ryan had seen that look before and it scared him. Roid-rage.

"I'm gonna kill that son of a bitch!" He headed for the door with Ryan and Avery following.

Outside they heard a snowmobile engine fire up, revving as it accelerated. They saw its lights cut across the field next to the house. Tyler ran toward the two remaining snowmobiles.

"Let him go, Tyler," Ryan shouted trying to hold him back. He shrugged Ryan off and started the snowmobile. Ryan managed to get on behind him as he gunned it and took off after Gavin. "Shit goddamnit!" Ryan clung to Tyler as he shifted to sit squarely on the seat.

"Wait up!" Avery climbed on the last snowmobile.

Jacob came running up to scramble on behind him. "I'm going with you."

Gavin had a good head start, but Tyler's Yamaha Phazer gained ground on him as he made his way toward the treacherous diamondback trail that scalloped the borders of Torch Lake. This trail had deep inclines and sharp corners built for only experienced snowmobile drivers. Tyler was decent and had a lot of experience but Ryan, Jacob and especially Avery had very little. Coming out of the corners they could see the flicker of red tail lights from Gavin's snowmobile. Ryan glanced over his shoulder. Avery was losing ground on them. Sliding side to side through the icy track the glow of his headlight was dwindling. Ryan felt Tyler shivering as he hung onto him but he knew it was with rage and not the cold. It was bad enough that Gavin had picked a fight in his father's cabin and done some damage to it; worse yet was his kicking Tyler in the face like that.

They made their descent down the steep part of the trail and still had no sign of the prick, but he was headed right toward the lake. He must've thought that he could out run them and then angle back toward the main road. Ryan remembered that last winter, near the end of this trail, Tyler had built a ramp for snowmobile jumping that veered at a 60° angle off to the left as if it headed back in the direction of the several fields along the road. As they got closer to it, Ryan knew that Gavin had no way of knowing about the ramp and if he took that offshoot he was in deep shit if he didn't line up properly for the narrow rise to the jump.

They came up on it and Tyler saw what Ryan did; the fresh deep ruts and cuts where Gavin's snowmobile had turned from the trail and was headed toward the ramp. Ryan looked back and saw the light from Avery and Jacob's snowmobile come around the turn. He saw Avery lift his head to spot them as Tyler goosed the throttle of their snowmobile shooting it down the new trail. In a minute, they were on top of him. He had hit the ramp too far to the right and shot into a cluster of pine trees and rocks that marked where just beyond the open fields began. His snowmobile lay there wrecked and as they plowed to a stop in a spray of snow, they saw him rising to his feet.

Cursing, Gavin walked toward them and pulled a large knife from his boot. He closed on them just as Avery and Jacob plowed to a stop in a shower of snow not far from him.

"Okay, motherfuckers we'll do this now if you want." He taunted Tyler and Ryan.

As they climbed off the Yamaha Ryan had grabbed Tyler by the arm to restrain him and drag him back. "Back off. We don't want any trouble." He looked at Gavin as he shoved Tyler behind him. "Tyler, let it go." He pivoted and put his hand on Tyler's chest and then half turned back to Gavin. "Get out of here... just go."

Avery and Jacob had come closer behind Gavin. "Hey, guys." Jacob stopped. He saw the gleam of the knife's blade in his hand. "Avery, watch out for th—" Avery had kept going a few steps and looked back at Jacob. Behind him, Gavin ran toward him slashing with the knife.

"Watch out!" Ryan cried out as Avery spun to the side to avoid it. Jacob stepped up and punched Gavin straight to the side of his head. It twisted him to the side and Jacob followed up with a kick at Gavin's knife hand connecting solidly. But he didn't drop the blade, instead slashing and slicing through the sleeve of Jacob's parka as he dodged away. But that brought him closer to Avery, who landed a punch to the back of his neck, knocking him down. Gavin rose to his knees and with a scream charged forward stabbing with the knife and narrowly missing Ryan's midsection who cracked him again on the side of his face. Gavin whirled around with the blade extended like a scythe as Tyler rushed past Ryan and ducked under Gavin's thrust while grabbing at a large stone from a nearby pile. As Gavin turned back to him he swung and the uppercut, the rock in his hand, connected with Gavin's throat and then jaw. They heard the crunch of bone and shattered teeth as Gavin's mouth and nose sprayed blood.

"Jesus Christ!" Avery cried.

Tyler walked over and kicked Gavin in the face with a more sickening crunch of flesh and cartilage. "How's that feel motherfucker?"

Ryan grabbed him and dragged him away. "He's not moving Tyler."

Avery knelt over the body. "I think he's fucking dead." He looked up at Ryan and Jacob with a wide-eyed wild look. "What the fuck are we going to do?"

"He's not dead." Tyler walked over and kicked Gavin's still form in the ribs. All it did was to knock snow from it where it had settled. "He's just a drug dealer and no one's going to care if someone beat the fucker up."

"He ain't moving." Avery staggered to his feet.

Jacob knelt and took the glove from his right hand. With a grimace, he touched the blood-soaked throat to check. He couldn't look at the ruin of Gavin's lower face. "I don't feel a pulse." He put the hand on his chest and leaned down. "He's not breathing." Jacob wiped his hand on his jacket using a handful of snow to scrub the blood from his fingers. "Fuck." He rose and backed away from the body.

"He's a scumbag dealer," Tyler repeated. "No one is going to give a shit what happened to him."

"Yeah, a dealer that you bought shit from." Ryan stared at Tyler. "That we fought with in front of people. And now we've killed him. The police are sure going to give a shit."

"It was self-defense, man. He came after me with a knife." Tyler looked less certain now.

Ryan shook his head. "You chased him down and then we confronted him. They're not gonna call that self-defense." Sobriety came in an instant as adrenaline burned the drugs from their polluted bodies. "Fuck!" Ryan said.

Jacob was pacing up and down looking at the body on the ground. "This will ruin us."

Tyler bent over it and checked for a pulse again. He shook his head as he stood.

"I can't believe this," Ryan's mouth was dry and he could barely say the words. "This'll wreck us!"

"What are we going to do?" Jacob looked at Ryan, Avery and then Tyler. "Maybe we should call our parents."

"And tell them what?" Tyler wanted to know. "That we beat this guy to death because we were still pissed at losing a football game!" There it was... that anger that had been simmering since the game's end. "Our parents can't get us out of this one." He shook his head and looked each of them in the eye. "We tell the truth and we are fucked." Tyler grabbed the body and started dragging him toward the rocky point and the drop off.

"What the fuck are you doing?" Ryan asked grabbing his arm to make him stop.

Jacob rubbed a hand across his face. "Maybe we should go back and call the police!"

"We can't say it was just an accident." Ryan looked at the bloodied remnants of Gavin's jaw and mouth and then away—he thought he was going to throw up. The jaw that once housed Gavin's teeth was shattered. The left side was completely out of the socket and detached from his skull. His neck and lower face still oozed blood and his mouth was full of teeth fragments. The snow beneath him slowly turned into a crimson slush. "His injuries... They don't look like something that would happen if he just dumped a snowmobile off a ramp and we found him like this."

Avery walked over and looked down at the body. "We can't just bury him. Something will dig him up."

"Let's put him under the ice." Tyler looked over his shoulder toward the lake. "If his body is ever found maybe nothing will match up."

They had unconsciously formed the corners of a square with the body in the middle. All four looked at each other. Within a single day, they had gone from expecting a victory in a game they'd played football most of their lives to win... to losing it... to killing a man. Now, it was all about survival and protecting their futures. Do they take their chances with the cops coming to an accident scene and it becoming clear that one of them had killed Gavin? Or do they get rid of his body, bury this secret deep, and hope they'd eliminated the possibility of any connection?

Tyler moved from his corner to stand over the body. "We need to all agree on this. We are going to come up with a story that each of us can repeat without any deviation. Or we will all be fucked." He looked each of them in the eye waiting for their nod. "We all agree that we are going to put him in the water and take our chances he'll never be found. And if he is, no matter when we tell everyone—I mean everyone—that we don't know anything about it. That we chased him but never caught up with him." He looked at Ryan, then Avery and Jacob. "Do you all agree?"

"Get rid of him." Ryan nodded toward the lake.

Avery's face looked as pale as the rest of theirs. "Put him under."

"Shit!" Jacob stared at the body. "The water..." He turned away from them.

Tyler bent and grabbed both legs. "Help me out here." The dead weight of a grown man of Gavin's size was hard to manage even for someone as strong as Tyler.

Avery and Ryan each took an arm. They carried the body to the water's edge. There was a skin of ice covering the majority of the lake. In sections, it was already inches thick.

"We need to get him out far enough and under deep enough so the current will draw him away from this spot." Tyler looked at the others who hadn't moved. "I told you. He's a fucking drug dealer <u>and</u> no one's going to miss him." He stopped at the edge. "Stuff his jacket and pockets full of rocks."

"Shit. Shit." Avery was breathing hard, but knelt to grab stones and hand them to Tyler. He saw Tyler feel around and then pull something, a gleam of metal in the snowmobile headlights—maybe a key—from Gavin's front pocket and put it in his own. He reached behind the body and pulled a wallet from the hip pocket. "We gotta get rid of this so they can't immediately identify him." He stuck it in his jacket pocket.

Ryan shook his head but knelt to help them. "We're fucked. We are so fucked."

They broke the ice on the water just a foot or so beneath the ledge. They picked the body up and lowered into the water on the side of the promontory where the current should take him away. As they lay flat to reach down and push the body under Ryan noticed Gavin's eyelids flutter and it seemed his hand twitched. Beside him he heard Avery's gasp.

"Oh fuck. Oh shit..."

Tyler swung around to hang his legs over the ledge and told Ryan. "Hold on to me." He slid off putting his full weight on the body, his feet square in its midsection, to push it completely underwater and outwards to slide it under the sheet of thicker ice. Ryan and Avery pulled him up. He was breathing heavily. "No one will ever miss him."

It was done. There they were, each not knowing if Gavin might have still been alive. They stood there on the shoreline sick about what they had done... disgusted at what they were doing. One thing was for sure. Any thoughts of reporting what had happened were over.

Ryan asked Tyler. "You checked his pulse, right? He was dead."

"Yeah. Yeah. That twitch... it was probably some after death body thing."

"What are we going to do now?" They turned to look at Jacob.

The snow was falling harder. Ryan looked up at the flakes and felt them touch and melt on his flushed face.

"Oh my God, I'm gonna be sick." Avery bent and vomited. Steam rose from the chunks.

"We have to all be on the same page," Tyler said. "Nobody can waiver from our story."

Ryan took a deep breath and agreed. "He's right. We have to be solid. Even if they don't find the body... if someone files a missing person report, I'm sure we're all going to be questioned at some point. So we have to be consistent in what we tell them; anyone that asks us. We tell them that yeah there was a fight with Gavin and we chased him when he stole the snowmobile. And that we caught up with the snowmobile, it was turned over—wrecked. That's all true. But, we found it in the field and never saw Gavin. Just his tracks running toward the road."

"That sounds good. It's simple and straightforward." Tyler and Avery nodded.

"Jacob?" Ryan looked at him.

"I got it—that's the story." He nodded once his mouth compressed into a tight thin line.

Tyler moved away from the edge of the lake. "Okay, let's go. Remember we stick to the story no matter what. Even if the cops get involved and try and turn it around on us and claim that one of us has said something or is telling a different story. We don't believe that shit. We never change the story ever. For the rest of our lives. Agreed?" He held his hand out as if it was a pregame huddle. "Til the end. Right!" Those were the words that had broken every team huddle since junior high school.

The others put their hand in. "Til the end."

Using pine needle-covered branches from nearby trees and their parkas they swept the snow clean and smoothed the area around them from what had happened. Tyler took one snowmobile and made tracks to the middle of the nearest open field closest to the road and then created divots in the snow as if someone not used to snowmobiles and unfamiliar terrain might have turned one over. Ryan, Avery, and Jacob had followed to leave another set of tracks and to set the scene to look like they had found and righted the snowmobile to tow it back to the cabin. They made their way back to the lake house and the roar of the snowmobile, one laboring as it towed the other, didn't drown out the chatter in their racing minds.

Ryan kept thinking, are we going to end up in jail? Stick to the plan… stick to the plan… and everything will be fine. As they got off the snowmobiles at the cabin it was dark and quiet. Tyler went to the still burning fire and emptied the wallet's contents and then tossed it into the center, hottest, part of the flames. For a moment they watched it burn and shrivel to a black lump that Tyler poked with a stick until its ashes fell apart. They heard footsteps behind them as Amanda and Shelley came from the cabin.

"Everyone else took off after the fight. They decided not to stick around." Amanda said not looking at Ryan.

"I cleaned up for you." Shelley smiled hesitantly and gave Amanda a look. "You guys were gone for a long time. Did you catch that guy? What an asshole, huh."

Tyler walked over and put his arm around her waist. "No. The fucker left the snowmobile he stole wrecked in the field. He must've run for the road. By the time we caught up with where he had dumped the snowmobile he was gone. We searched but never found him."

Amanda looked at him but his eyes shifted away. She turned to Ryan, who didn't say anything to her. She walked off to one of the bedrooms.

"I don't know why she is so pissed." Shelley shrugged.

Tyler went to the kitchen and came back with four beers tossing one to each of them. They drank and no one said a word. Shelley looked around and seemed puzzled. "You guys are so quiet."

Tyler pinched her on the ass and she squealed. "Well, it's been a hell of a day." He grabbed at her. "But I still got some energy left."

"Doesn't your nose hurt?" Shelly gingerly touched it.

"Yeah, but I don't need it tonight." He took her hand and led her to the bedroom.

Not looking at Avery and Jacob as they went to their room Ryan headed to bed. But he couldn't get his brain to stop spinning with all that had happened. All he could think was, I'm gonna have to go to bed each night worrying that the next morning could be a disaster of facing cops pounding on the door demanding answers. To questions none of us wanted to face. About a terrible thing we had done and had to hold inside for the rest of our lives. He took a bottle out of the bag beside his bed and twisted the cap off and raised it to his lips. Drink... drink... into darkness.

* * *

As the others finally slept just before daybreak, Tyler crossed the field next to the house following the original straight line of the tracks from Gavin's snowmobile. He continued past where Gavin had turned back toward the lake trying to shake them. On the other side of the field was a dirt road. Tyler found where he had parked his truck on the side of the road near the drive up to the house. Leaving it there must have been easier than trying to back out if he ended up leaving in a hurry. Tyler thought, the fucker sure knew he was going to have to make a fast exit. He moved the truck further down the road angling it off the side and into the woods. Checking to make sure he didn't have a spare he took out a knife and slashed a tire as if it had been punctured. Fifteen minutes later he was coming up the driveway, hands deep in his parka with his head down, and nearly back at the cabin.

"Find something out there?" Tyler looked up. It was Avery.

"Thought I'd check to see if he'd left a car out there. I pushed his truck off the road and into the woods and gave it a flat tire to look like he'd had to leave it there since he didn't have a spare."

* * *

Ryan woke with dry eyes and a sandpaper mouth. He stepped out of the bedroom and saw the busted frame of the stained glass window. He rubbed his eyes but they still burned. It hadn't been a dream. It had really happened. How he wished it'd all been a nightmare. He went to the kitchen. Jacob walked in and he could tell he felt the same way. His heart fell into his stomach and his pulse surged as he looked at him. He became paralyzed by fear and all he could think about was, stick to the plan—stick to the plan. Tyler and Avery came in. As they sat at the table, Avery looked at Tyler for a moment, as if studying him. They all looked preoccupied with thoughts of what had happened the night before. Each could see it in the quick, haunted, glances into each other's eyes and then away.

"Before we leave you should tape up the busted window in the front door," Jacob commented. "We could cut a piece of cardboard from one of the boxes in the pantry and put over it." He didn't wait for Tyler to answer and stood up. "I'll take care of it."

"I'll help you." Avery said and left with a last look at Tyler.

"What's up with you and Avery?" Ryan asked Tyler.

He shrugged. "Nothing."

Chapter 7

TORCH LAKE
THE JENNELO'S LAKE CABIN

"Come on Amanda ride with me." It was late Sunday morning and they were gathering their things for the trip back home. Ryan stopped her as she was putting her bags in Shelley's red Toyota Celica Liftback.

She shook off his hand. "No. I'm going with Shelley."

Amanda had barely talked to him since the fight. The morning after they had all been silently lost in their own thoughts. Ryan had followed her into the cabin to the bedroom. She grabbed her bathroom bag of shampoo and cosmetics. He was in the doorway. She waited for him to move and when he didn't, "Okay." She set the bag at her feet and put her hands on her hips. "Tell me what's going on."

"I'm sorry about that girl showing up." Ryan reached for her and she stepped back.

"You told me you were with her while we were broken up. Okay, that hurt. But okay." She had tears in her eyes. "But that other stuff that you and Tyler are into—I asked you to stop."

Ryan nodded. "And I didn't listen to you then." He thought of what had happened at the lake's edge and wondered how much of it had been fueled by steroids and drugs that released their rage at losing the game. If they had won would they have just blown it off and let him go?

"You lied to me, Ryan. You said you would... you said you had. But you didn't." she turned her back to him.

"But it's over, Amanda. Never again. I promise." He moved closer and touched her shoulder to get her to look at him.

"What happened with that guy that came after you?" She was still upset but willing to let go of that part of her concern about his lie and about that girl, Kelly.

"It was just a fight."

She shook her head. "No. Afterward. You guys looked scared when you came back." She stepped forward and he backed up clearing the doorway. "What happened?"

"Nothing. Nothing happened." He looked away. "We found where he'd wrecked and left the snowmobile. We never saw him."

She waited in silence until his eyes returned to hers. "Something happened with that guy... I know it, Ryan." She watched him shake his head and then continued. "What are you going to do about that girl, about Kelly?" She waited but he didn't say anything. She picked up her bag and put it in the trunk and closed it. "I'm riding with Shelley."

* * *

The long drive south was as quiet as the prior day's travel north. Getting over the loss of their childhood dream seemed minuscule compared to the potential murder charge hanging over them. Inside the Shelby Township city limits, they exited the slick highway in Tyler's rear-wheel drive, Trans Am and made their way to Avery's house. As they pulled into his driveway, Ryan leaned over to the center console with his hand out and stated. "We're all good on this, right?" He quickly saw three other hands connect with his. "Til the end."

Avery got out and leaned down to look in the window. "Later guys."

Then they dropped off Jacob who got out of the car without saying anything. And then Tyler stopped at his house. Ryan looked at him and he nodded. "We had to do it, man. It was that or we were all fucked." Tyler touched his swollen nose. "I'll tell my dad that I'm the one who wrecked the snowmobile."

Ryan nodded at him and got out but in his mind he couldn't help but think that no matter what they were all potentially fucked anyway. They would have to live that way, with that possibility hanging over their heads, maybe for the rest of their lives. Ryan wondered how each of them was going to be able to process what had happened and to live with it.

* * *

RYAN KRAMER'S HOUSE

He went in his house and quietly shut the door behind him. Ryan heard his mother's voice come from the kitchen. "I saw Tyler pull in. How was your time up north?" She came out of the kitchen wiping her hands on a rag. "I was worried about you guys going up there so soon after that game. I know how devastated you were after losing."

"Everything was good. We're fine mom." He took his jacket off and hung it on the peg just inside the kitchen door and tossed his bag in the laundry room.

She stood there looking up at him and he could see the questioning look on her face. He almost panicked at what he thought she was going to ask.

"You boys cleaned up before you left and didn't leave things a mess, right?"

He let out a breath he didn't realize he had been holding. "Yeah, mom. We didn't leave a mess."

She walked to him with still-damp hands, reached up, and patted him on the cheek. "You must be tired. You look it. Why don't you go up and lay down for a while and rest?" Her smile was the same as it always been as far back as he could remember. Sweet and caring, full of love. Ryan wondered how she would feel about him if she found out what had happened.

"I think I will." He leaned down and gave her a kiss. He went to his room only to realize that, not counting Amanda, his mom was the first of many times he would have to cover up one thing after another about the day of his final high school football game. He couldn't tell his mother or father anything. Because even if he told them the story they had come up with, it would still lead to more questions. They wouldn't just let it go.

He laid down on his bed and closed his eyes. But they quickly popped open. He worried if they had done a good enough job covering the tracks at the lake. There had been a lot of blood where they had killed Gavin and sunk his body under the ice. Did they get it all from the crime scene? And did those new tracks look convincing? The ones into the center of the field to look like they had found and then towed the snowmobile Gavin crashed from there back to the cabin. Shit! Did he have any blood on his dirty clothes in the bag he had left downstairs in the laundry room? Was his mom emptying the bag now and looking at blood smears wondering where they were from? He was freaking out even though he knew he had double checked that as he packed before they left the cabin. Then he wondered about Tyler, Avery and Jacob's clothes. Did they think to check theirs? His brain wouldn't stop. He jumped out of bed. He couldn't sleep as his mind raced from one 'what if' to another—they seemed endless.

He looked out his bedroom window at the overcast, late afternoon, sky and wondered if the rest of his life would be spent hiding from the truth of one bad event—one tragic mistake—made on a single day. Covering up one thing after another day after day. As he watched, the gray sky darkened into evening and he couldn't sit there any longer. Grabbing his wallet and car keys he went downstairs.

"Mom, I forgot to give Tyler something. I'll be back in a couple of hours." He went out the door in a hurry to his Monte Carlo before she could reply.

Chapter 8

TYLER JENNELO'S HOUSE

Ryan needed to convince Tyler they needed to tell his father what really happened—about the fight but not what they had done to Gavin. It was better if they were the ones to tell him. He pulled into Tyler's driveway and honked the horn once as he got out. It was their signal for Tyler to meet him at the door. He opened it as Ryan walked up the sidewalk from the driveway and stepped outside.

Ryan joined him on the porch. "We need to go ahead and tell your dad about the fight. By tomorrow you know that one of our friends is gonna talk and news of the fight will get around to him."

"He just got home so I haven't said anything yet." Tyler nodded at him to come in.

Inside they saw Mr. Jennelo setting his briefcase on the desk in his office. He smiled when he saw Ryan and waved them in.

He shook Ryan's hand. "I know losing that game was hard but I hope you boys had fun up north. Come spring time we'll go up for a long week and let you boys use the boat to spend some time on the lake. It's beautiful up there."

"Thanks, sir, but I have something to tell you that happened at your cabin and it was my fault."

Rick Jennelo looked from Ryan to his son's swollen nose and the bruise under his black eyes. "I thought there might be a story coming when I saw Tyler's face." His smile had flattened as he looked back to Ryan. "Well?"

"Mr. Jennelo, some friends heard about us being up there and just showed up."

"Friends?" he looked again at Tyler's face then back at me.

"There was a fight. It was with some guy—not one of our friends—who showed up, too and was mad at me. He thought I'd been with his girlfriend and attacked me. Tyler tried to get him off me." Ryan looked at Tyler then back at his father. "It's not Tyler's fault. It was mine and I'll pay for the busted stuff." Ryan could see that irritated look forming on Mr. Jennelo's face. Tyler had inherited it. "We're sorry about the party.

"Who's this other boy?" He looked again at his son. "He from up there or around here?"

Tyler shook his head. "He's not a boy—he's some drug dealer, dad."

"How do you know that?" He looked at Tyler and then when he didn't get a response from him he glared at Ryan.

"We've heard about him, Mr. Jennelo," Ryan told him. "Around town. He comes over from the city."

"And you say after the fight he took off?"

Tyler nodded. "We chased him, Dad. Didn't catch him but found the snowmobile he'd stolen to get away from us. It was wrecked. There were tracks from it to the road." Tyler shrugged. "We think he caught a ride or someone was there waiting for him."

Mr. Jennelo now looked less pissed off. "Thanks for telling me Ryan. I appreciate you taking responsibility." He glanced at Tyler then back to Ryan. "Don't worry about it. It's getting late and you should get home."

* * *

A couple of hours later, Tyler heard his father close the French doors to his office and then his steps climbing the stairs to his bedroom. He waited another 20 minutes before sneaking downstairs through the kitchen and out the back door to the side yard and through the gate and onto the street. It was four miles to Silver's Gym—its proximity was one reason he had picked it for his workouts this past summer— an easy 30-minute run. He had already stretched so he took off down the sidewalk that paralleled the street.

Twenty-six minutes later, breathing deeply but evenly, he bent to unlock the employee entrance door at the back of the building. Tony Silva, the owner who had named his place Silver's as a play on Gold's Gym, was a big Eisenhower Eagles booster. He had given Tyler a key and security code so he could come in and work out any time he wanted whether late in the evening or early in the morning. He went through the storeroom toward the front of the gym and turned left into the locker and dressing room area. Taking a pair of gloves from his backpack, he got out the key he had recognized in Gavin's pocket for locker number 17.

That summer in his dealings with Gavin to get his steroids, he had seen him take them from a bag in his locker and put the money back into it. He turned the key and opened the door to that rank, sour sweat smell he was so familiar with. The bag was underneath a pile of nasty, soiled, workout clothes. He pulled it out, unzipped, and looked inside. There were some steroids, which was what he was after but also bags of white powder and several stacks of green bills strapped together. Holy shit! He thumbed through it to get a quick count. Holy shit!

He quickly emptied the bag into his backpack and put his towel, ball cap and water bottle back in on top of it. Closing the backpack, he slung it onto his shoulders. He took Gavin's now empty bag and filled it with the dirty clothes and put it back in the locker closed and locked it. After stripping his gloves off he stuffed them in his windbreaker pocket.

He made the run home in 25 minutes. Back in his room, he flipped his mattress over to reveal the square that he had cut out a year ago to stash his steroids and marijuana. He stuffed the money and cocaine inside. It all fit and he put the flap of material back in place to seal it in. He stretched out on the bed and felt the air current from the ceiling fan dry the sweat on his face and chest. He had counted the cash. $50,000. Holy shit!

Chapter 9

NOVEMBER 1988
RYAN KRAMER

Monday morning, I made my way through the school doors trying to avoid people and any conversation. I didn't want to hear any, "Hey Ryan, too bad about that game. I thought you guys had them beat." I didn't want sympathetic bullshit from anybody regarding the game or any questions about the fight up north.

I didn't go out of my way looking for Amanda, but waited for her to find me. By lunch time, I was sure she was absent. I went outside and her white LeBaron was not in the senior parking lot which was almost a sense of relief since I knew Amanda would be my next thing I'd have to deal with.

The day was full of a constant, hollow, background noise of teachers lecturing on nothing my mind was capable of absorbing. All I could do is stay within myself and stare at the second hand of the clock. Every time it passed 12 it felt like one more step away from the trouble up north. Full of anxiety and lack of sleep I was pulling away from reality.

A head bob was about all I could give anyone who tried to make conversation with me. I was sinking deeper into my mind, closing off anything that might expose our secret. The next two days were much of the same leading up to Thanksgiving. Still no Amanda at school and my fascination with the clock continued.

Each night the illumination of the red digits on my alarm clock were slowly stripping layer upon layer from my tired eyes. As horrible as insomnia was, the worst was that it started to feel as if I was numbly looking down at myself through a fog and all I saw was an empty shell. I felt the absence of a soul; there was nothing inside the body of Ryan Kramer and I was drifting toward an unknown and hidden place.

I had read a lot about it and knew, psychologically, I was trying to escape the truth. Was Gavin really alive when we sank his body? I went far down the path of trying to convince myself that he was already dead when we shoved him in the water. Even with all the sleepless nights and countless replays of what went down, every effort to convince myself that what happened to Gavin hadn't were to no avail.

Was I a stone cold killer? If I shifted my mind and accepted what I saw, then he was still alive when we put him under the ice. Fuck! It was time to hit my dad's liquor cabinet again. Chivas Regal, man, does this shit taste bad. What did I do—what did we all do? Take a drink. When are they coming for me? Drink again. When were they coming for all of us? Drink more. My life will never be the same. It's 4:44 AM. Sorry, Amanda for what I've done. Drink even more. Where the hell is Kelly and what does she know about what happened to Gavin? Here I am drinking on fucking Thanksgiving weekend when we should be playing in the Silverdome. I continued to hit the fifth of booze but I was only able to anesthetize myself for three hours.

Later that morning, our annual Thanksgiving party was starting. Family guests began to pour in for the day's events; a large feast held at the halftime of the Lions game. I reluctantly made light conversation with aunts, uncles, and cousins. We consumed large quantities of food long into the fourth quarter of the game. The Lions looked terrible as usual as they got thumped by Minnesota 23 to 0.

Sitting in the kitchen after the game I could hear my father's voice over the sounds of crashing, dirty, dishes hitting the sink.

"Ryan get in here."

As I approached the living room, I could hear the voice of a reporter on TV. It was Diana Lewis, Action News. I entered the room and could see the picture on the television with an announcement at the bottom: Body Found at Torch Lake!

My father grabbed my arm and pulled me upstairs to my room. "You came back from up north awful quiet. Did you hear anything about this? They found a man in the water up there, at Torch Lake."

Maybe it was a lack of sleep or maybe I was still buzzed from all the drinking earlier in the morning. I knew he wouldn't hear about the fight as quickly as Tyler's dad but he would at some point. A certain calmness came over me as I began to tell my father the story we had agreed upon.

"Dad, after the game we had a party at Tyler's father's lake cabin. Some guy showed up there mad and confronted me saying I had been with his girlfriend over the summer. He started a fight with me."

"What happened, Ryan?"

"I hit him a few times and then Tyler got involved and the guy kicked him in the face breaking his nose. Then he ran, stealing one of Tyler's father's snowmobiles. We chased after him only to find the snowmobile he'd stolen had been left wrecked in a field but we never saw him again."

"I wonder who the guy is that they found in the lake?" My dad was still concerned.

"I don't know. The guy we were chasing… his name was Gavin. Have they identified the body?"

My father shook his head. "I haven't heard, yet. And you say you boys never saw him again, right?" He stopped. Someone downstairs had turned the TV up and the reporter was talking again. "Police have not identified the body and that's all we have right now. We'll update you again with more as soon as we have it. This is Diana Lewis reporting for Action News from Torch Lake."

"Why didn't you tell me about all of this after it happened?" He asked me.

"I didn't want you to be pissed at me." I grabbed his shoulder. "He started the fight, Dad but he ran off and we never saw him again. If that's his body, I don't know how he ended up in the lake." I sat on my bed and wanted to puke. I had to choke it down.

"Who knows you and Tyler had a fight with this guy that disappeared?"

I shrugged. "Maybe a dozen of our friends."

My father headed downstairs. I heard him call out to his brother who was an attorney in Ann Arbor. Within minutes, I felt a hand on my shoulder and looked up. It was my uncle. I didn't need to repeat our lie to him—that we'd done nothing to Gavin—my dad did that for me.

"Don't say anything to anyone about this and I'll talk with a few criminal defense colleagues." He followed my father from my room.

Later that day as our guests left the house my only thought was that this was the story I will have to live and die with no matter how twisted my mind gets. Coming clean will never be an option. This will always be on my shoulders for the sake of myself and my three best friends.

The weekend was filled with my father fielding phone calls from my uncle behind closed doors. I called Tyler, Jacob, and Avery to let them know my parents now knew and my uncle, the lawyer, was aware of the fight, as well. I suggested that Jacob and Avery tell their families to make them aware of any breaking news or contact from the police. I went over the exact story we had agreed on before to make sure nothing had changed or was omitted. If we stuck with that no one would ever connect the body to us or suspect, we were involved in anything. They were all freaked out but understood this was our plan until the end.

My father was in favor of telling the authorities about the fight with Gavin at Torch Lake. However, my uncle's legal advice was to keep quiet unless the law came calling. I guess innocence is looked at in a better light if things are unknown. It was much better to ask forgiveness for not immediately coming forward about the fight than to stir things prematurely.

Telling my father all of the events piece by piece to match our story settled my nerves enough to allow me to get over that night's biggest hurdle. I had to persuade myself into only thinking that our story was a reality. Blocking out the last segment of Gavin's bloodied face and battered body would not be easy but the only way I could make our story credible. Any thoughts of the final moments of our encounter were discarded or dismissed as only a possible scenario that could've taken place. I was prepared to say, "I sure am glad we never caught up with him or something bad might have happened." That was as much as I, and I hoped the others, would admit.

* * *

The day of the state championship came and I picked up Jacob, Tyler, and Avery to make the kickoff at 1:00 PM at the Pontiac Silverdome. Catholic Central was set to play Traverse City for the Class A title. The game that we thought would be our childhood defining moment.

Instead, it was one last opportunity to solidify our story and plan for anything that might come our way. Everyone was on the same page right down to the last minute of every segment of the night at Torch Lake. I was amazed at how each had such a smooth take on everything. One thing that was not clear was how they would perceive things when the demons came calling in the night. Something I don't think anyone wanted to discuss but would everyone be able to handle the mental torment? I didn't want to discuss my coping skills for fear that my three best friends would feel they were in the company of a psychopath. They're strong and will get through it, I convinced myself.

The game flew by and Traverse City put our former foe, Catholic Central, away in convincing fashion. The only thought we had was, damn I wish we had those bastards on turf and the title would've been ours. Those thoughts were short-lived and seemed unimportant with our own impending criminal and legal battle possibly going to begin.

* * *

UTICA EISENHOWER HIGH SCHOOL

That Monday morning came and things felt somewhat back to normal. I thought that maybe enough time would pass and a normal life would resume. It's strange how we can trick our mind into an altered perception of reality when it serves our purpose.

Unfortunately, convincing my soul I fear will be impossible. Nonetheless, this was the hand I must play until the end of my days.

As I entered the school parking lot, I saw her there standing next to her car with her arms crossed watching me pull in. Amanda was ready for a confrontation. I closed my car door and grabbed my bag. All I could think of was, here we go.

"How could you do this to me, Ryan? You knock up some girl you don't even know and you can't tell me what you're going to do about it. About her or the baby." She paced back and forth in front of me and then stopped. "I mean how could you... with her. She's.... she's not me. Was it just because she'd let you screw her?"

I saw a group of juniors watching us. I scowled at them and they started walking toward the school. Amanda and I had already gone through this before leaving Torch Lake. I hadn't had an answer for her questions then and didn't have one now. Well, I did, but the real answer was because I was wasted and Kelly was an easy lay. I couldn't tell that to Amanda and couldn't think of what to say to her right now as she cried uncontrollably. I wrapped my arms around her and held her tight. She twisted to look up at me and the anger changed to a concerned look on her face. "What the hell happened after I left that night? You wouldn't tell me the next morning but something happened."

Keep to the story. Keep to the story... went through my mind. I replayed what we had rehearsed as I walked her through the school doors. Saved by the bell. She quickly separated from me leaving me with a sense of how badly I had failed and ruined a wonderful connection with her.

* * *

MID-DECEMBER 1988
KROGER STOCK ROOM
SHELBY TOWNSHIP

Ryan was lifting the box to the top shelf when Jacob slapped his shoulder and said, "It's her."

He turned to see Kelly come in by climbing through the open roll-up door of the dock using the slack length of chain to pull herself up. Ryan gave the box a final one-handed shove to make sure it was squarely on the shelf. He looked around to see if any of the other stockers or bag boys were around.

"Where is he?" She looked even worse than the night at Torch Lake. Ryan was sure she was coming off something. He could see the spasms of withdrawal that crawled through her. They could hear it in the strain in her voice, too. "Where's Gavin?"

Jacob looked at Ryan, who gave a little left right headshake that he took as don't say anything.

Her arms, hands stuffed into her coat pockets, stiffened with a jerk. "I haven't seen him in weeks." Her voice raised. "I know he followed me—I know what happened up there." She came closer and they could see the cold-sweat shine on her face. "I can't get by without... he's got my..." she shuddered.

"We didn't see him after he took off, Kelly." Ryan bent to pick up another box turning his back to her.

"I'm giving you a chance to tell me what happened to Gavin and some time to think about doing the right thing," She held her stomach and her eyes bored into Ryan's when he looked up. "But if you don't then I'm going to the police." She took her hands out of the pockets and rubbed her face.

Ryan straightened and faced her. "He jumped me and kicked Tyler in the face. Yeah, we chased him when he ran. And we found the snowmobile he had stolen and wrecked. Good thing he ran off or we would have kicked his ass. But we never saw him, Kelly." He put the box up on the shelf motioning to Jacob, "Come on let's get this finished." They both ignored her and after a couple minutes she left the way she came.

Jacob walked over to the dock and leaned out looking right and left. "She's gone." He looked at Ryan, who had joined him just inside the door. "Do you think she'll go to the cops?"

"I don't know." Ryan took the chain from its retention hook and pulled down on it to roll the door closed. "I hope not. We need to tell Tyler and Avery about her showing up and asking questions."

Chapter 10

RYAN KRAMER'S HOUSE

They met at Ryan's house. Tyler looked nervous, which was rare for him. Avery still seemed withdrawn as if he didn't want to be around his friends. Jacob was quiet. He had more to lose than any of them. He had been approached by several major colleges around the country offering him a full scholarship and had committed to USC. Something like this could make that all disappear.

"So what," Tyler said. "She doesn't know anything because she wasn't there when it happened. Eddie saw her get in a car and take off minutes after she stomped out of the cabin. She was gone when Gavin got there."

"Well maybe she wasn't there, but she sure seems intent on stirring shit up," Jacob said. "I mean she seems determined to find out where Gavin is." He looked at Tyler, who crossed his arms and frowned.

"I don't know what to do with her about that," Ryan said. "As for the other thing she has on me—that I slept with her—yeah I did. But I don't know for certain that I'm the father or that she really is pregnant. She might have been shaking me down for money to buy drugs. So aside from that, there's nothing really that she can go after us with."

Avery didn't look up, or at them, as he commented. "All she's got to do is go to the police and file a report and raise a ruckus." He looked up at Tyler. "Then, even if Gavin's a drug dealer, eventually they're going to have to look into it."

* * *

JANUARY 1989
DETROIT METRO POLICE DEPARTMENT PRECINCT

Kelly sat in one of the side rooms facing the sergeant who was to take her statement.

"Okay, you haven't seen him for several weeks. Where did you last see your boyfriend?" He didn't seem the least interested but picked up his pen and notepad.

"At our place, Forest Apartments. But other people saw him up north at a cabin on Torch Lake afterward."

"How do you know that?"

"I was up there, too. But just before he was." She shifted in the chair.

The sergeant rubbed the tip of his nose with his pencil eraser and then added a note to the report sheet. "But, if I understand you correctly, you say you didn't see him there."

"I just told you that I was up there before he was. I had left before he showed up."

"If you were boyfriend and girlfriend—together as a couple— why did you travel separately?"

"What does that have to do with him being missing?" She didn't like being around cops.

"Everything I ask in this process is for a reason, miss. Please answer the question."

"I had to go alone but he followed me up there."

"It sounds like that was something you didn't want or didn't expect. Was there a reason why you went up there alone, without him?"

Kelly shook her head. "How is asking stuff about me going to help find Gavin?" She crossed her thin arms and glared at the sergeant. The door opened and another police officer came in and handed the sergeant a folder. He took it and flipped through the pages. She caught a glimpse of a photo—a mug shot of her—clipped inside.

"You have quite a rap sheet here." The sergeant studied her. "Possession. Driving under the influence. Shoplifting. You're close to scoring some time behind bars." He gave her a flat look. "Why has it taken you so long to report him missing?"

She stiffened with anger. "Yeah, I've messed up some and I tried to find him on my own." Her face was even paler than when she had come in. "It's not easy for someone like me to come to the police. But I got a right to report when I think something's happened to someone. Don't I?"

The sergeant nodded and sighed. "You do." He pulled the notepad closer to him and wrote something down then looked up at her. "Okay. It's important that I learn about why your boyfriend followed you up north. The way you said it makes me think he suspected something. And that could be important to helping you find him."

Kelly took a deep breath. "We'd had a fight when he found out I was pregnant."

"Is he the father?"

She shook her head. "No. He and I had broken up and I... I was with another guy a couple of times."

"So he was mad."

"Yeah. Really mad. I think he knew who it was but I wouldn't tell him. Then I went up north to see the other guy—to tell him I was pregnant—and Gavin followed me."

The sergeant flipped the sheet to a new page. "Who were you going to see at Torch Lake?"

"A boy named Ryan Kramer."

"Does this Kramer boy live up there?"

"No he and his friends live just outside Detroit, over in Shelby, and they were at one of their dads' lake cabin for the weekend."

"So you confronted this Ryan Kramer and what happened?"

"I told him I was pregnant and that he was the father and we had some words. Then his friends got involved and I left."

"That was it?"

"Yeah. I heard, back down here, from some people the next day that Gavin showed up there right after I left."

"What happened then?"

"I guess Gavin and Ryan got in a fight, that's what I heard, and then Ryan's friend Tyler was in on it, too. Then Gavin took off and Ryan and his friends chased him. No one has seen him since then." She felt her gut wrench because she knew what the next question would be and despite what she'd told them at Torch Lake, she hadn't wanted to narc on them.

"You said this Ryan Kramer and his friends live in Metro Detroit. I need their names and addresses if you have it."

"I don't know their addresses but their names are Ryan Kramer, Tyler Jennelo, Jacob Winslow and Avery Irons. They're all seniors at Utica Eisenhower High School."

The sergeant scratched his nose again with the pencil. "A couple of those names sound familiar... Jennelo and something about that Winslow boy."

"They're all football stars."

The sergeant seemed more interested. "That's it... the Winslow kid—the Eagles quarterback—he's headed to USC. Right?"

Kelly shrugged her shoulders. "I don't care. I just want to find out where Gavin is."

The sergeant looked at her and nodded. "Did you see the news a few weeks ago about up at Torch Lake?"

"What news?" Kelly looked puzzled and shook her head.

The officer stood and gestured for her to stand, too. "Would you be willing to look at a body that was found up there by the Antrim County Sheriff's department and see if you can identify it?"

* * *

JANUARY 1989
UTICA EISENHOWER HIGH SCHOOL

The school year quickly moved on but that stopped shortly after the holidays, in the new year, with a gut-wrenching lurch. During third period one day, I was summoned to the office. I hoped it was just another recruiter with a last minute scholarship offer as I made my way to the front of the school. Through the glass of the office's double doors, I could see three state troopers, in their dark blue uniforms, waiting for me. Before I could say anything, my uncle came out of the principal's office.

"Ryan, they've called your father and he's on his way. He called me and I got here first. They've identified that body as Gavin Murdoch—the boy you got into the fight with. Someone filed a missing report on him and that led to the identification." He lifted a hand and beckoned me to follow him inside into the principal's office.

The state troopers came in right behind us. Inside were the school principal, Mr. Burton, two Shelby Charter Township police officers in uniform and a man in a suit wearing a badge at his belt. My uncle introduced him.

"Ryan, this is Homicide Detective Lieutenant Horton from the Antrim County Sheriff's office. He needs to talk to you about what happened at Mr. Jennelo's house on Torch Lake." My uncle motioned at me to sit down in the chair that had been placed in front of them.

I broke the story down in every detail for them. We went over and over it and all seemed to come out clean. It was more like a fact-finding interview than an interrogation. Finishing my story with that we had never caught up to Gavin, I looked through the office window and saw Jacob outside. He must be waiting to be questioned next. The detective in the suit and the principal thanked me for the information. As I left, I noticed my uncle stayed inside. He must have talked to my friend's parents and was going to help navigate all of us through this process. Outside the door, before he went in, I looked Jacob straight in the eye and without words tried to convey a message. Stay strong.

Chapter 11

LATE JANUARY 1989
TORCH LAKE
THE JENNELO'S LAKE CABIN

The Police Lieutenant stood talking with the uniformed officer and made notes as the evidence technicians gathered their equipment. He put the small notebook in his back pocket and walked over to where Tyler and his father stood.

"Mr. Jennelo," he nodded to them.

"Yes, Lieutenant?" Tyler's father returned the nod.

The detective scratched an eyebrow and gave Tyler a look before focusing on his father. "Mr. Jennelo you say you had the damage repaired the day after your son told you about the fight."

"That's right."

"Then," he paused to scratch his eyebrow again. "Why didn't you report it to the police?" His hard stare shifted to drill Tyler then turned back to Rick Jennelo. "I mean calling it in when you found out. Instead, of it taking a missing person's report to bring us here."

"I didn't think it was important. It was just a couple of teenage boys fighting." He gestured at the repairs and shrugged. "It wasn't even much of a fight. And no big deal."

The detective looked at Tyler. "Metro PD in Detroit says they've had other calls about you." He held up his hand to Mr.

Jennelo, who had bristled at that. "No official complaints... but according to them, you got some temper." He waited for a response but didn't get one. "Don't you?"

Tyler didn't say anything but returned his stare. His father put his arm around his shoulders. He looked at the Lieutenant's ID. "Lieutenant Horton, my boy is high-spirited. He and his friends had just lost a football game that was pretty important to them."

The detective shook his head. "Not sure what that has to do with this." He looked at Tyler. "You knew this Gavin though he was a man a few years older than you, didn't you?

"You know I do since you've already talked to my friends and me." Tyler stared at him.

"And you said you met him while you and he worked out at the same gym this past summer?"

"I don't see the relevance. Wasn't he a known drug dealer Lieutenant?" Rick Jennelo asked. "That's likely got something to do with what happened to him."

The detective picked at his other eyebrow. "Maybe." He looked from Tyler to his father. "There's not much in here that shows anything." He gestured at the uniformed cop who came over and joined them. "Now why don't you show us where you found the snowmobile you said that this Gavin took."

They crossed the field and were soon at the spot that Tyler indicated. "This is it. Where we found the snowmobile. We couldn't find him though and towed the snowmobile back."

The Lieutenant scanned the field covered with a white blanket. The only marks on it were their own tracks from the cabin.

He walked a circle around the spot and then gestured at the uniformed cop who had brought along the two evidence technicians. He pointed an index finger up and twirled it in a spiraling motion. The uniform and the techs spread out in an expanding circle from where they stood. He turned to Tyler and his father. "Is there anything else that you can tell me?" Tyler shrugged and shook his head. "Well, then you two can go. We'll continue here and let you know if we find anything and need to talk to you further."

* * *

The heavy Mercedes sedan was quiet despite the snow tires. Once they were on the road, Rick Jennelo asked his son without looking at him. "Now, tell me what you didn't tell me before. I know you're hiding something."

"Okay." Tyler let out a deep breath and squirmed in the seat. "Gavin is the guy that supplied my steroids. And on top of that Ryan got his girlfriend pregnant. He was going to tell everything."

"What!" The Mercedes fishtailed and then steadied on the road.

It spilled from Tyler like he was purging everything in him. "We didn't mean to kill him, Dad! He went after us with a knife. It was an accident!" Tyler pleaded.

"Jesus fucking Christ!" Rick Jennelo exploded.

Chapter 12

**FEBRUARY 1989
AMANDA'S HOUSE
SHELBY TOWNSHIP**

"I called you and left messages," Ryan said.

Amanda twisted the charm bracelet he had given her their first Christmas together. She wore it on her right wrist and he knew that she did that when she had something to say but wasn't sure how to say it.

"We talked about driving to Florida after graduation before I leave for Cornell. Do you still want to do that?" He felt he had to ask her since it had been something they had planned but with what was going on between them he wasn't sure she would go. With what was going on he didn't know if he would be able to live up to it but he needed to know if she still had feelings for him.

She looked at him and he knew she was aware something was going on. Something beyond the steroid use and other drugs. She had forgiven him for what had happened with Kelly. That was a mistake he had made when they weren't together and she knew she shouldn't hold him accountable for that. But that didn't change facts about what had just happened, that she was about to tell him, that made how she felt even worse.

"Kelly Madison overdosed. My mom heard it from Lorraine down at the Sunset Country on Van Dyke; her sister's a nurse who works at Beaumont Hospital and told her about this poor young girl who'd been brought in. Mom asked her what the girl's name was and got the whole story. Kelly lost the baby the doctors discovered she was carrying."

Ryan felt like he had been punched in the gut but didn't know why. Kelly hadn't meant anything to him. Had she really been pregnant with his child? He looked at Amanda, who seemed to be waiting for him to say something. "Christ," was all that came out.

"I guess they'll keep her in the hospital for a while and then get her into some rehab program." She was still looking at him.

Ryan shook his head. He couldn't meet her eyes. "I don't know what to say."

"It's terrible—tragic." Amanda had tears in her eyes. "I don't know whether she was pregnant or not with your baby. That doesn't matter. Poor little thing. And I don't know if what she told the police, about you, Tyler, Jacob and Avery having something to do with what happened to her boyfriend is true or not." She shook her head and her long hair fell over her eyes and shrouded her face. She looked up at Ryan through the locks of her hair. "But I know that you and me. We... we can't be together. Not right now." She closed her eyes and whispered. "Please go."

Ryan stood and reached out a hand to touch her head bowed in front of him. She didn't move and he held it an inch above. That moment seemed an eternity. She didn't have anything more to say. He walked to the door and shut it quietly behind him.

Chapter 13

LETTER OF INTENT DAY, FEBRUARY 1989
UTICA EISENHOWER HIGH SCHOOL

"Coach, is that it? Is that all of the contact letters?" Tyler asked quietly.

Coach Murphy lifted his ball cap and scratched his bald scalp. "That's all I have." He touched the folder he had open on his desk. He looked at the four boys sitting across from him. They each had a letter in front of them; the best offer, in his estimation, they were going to receive from colleges and universities. "Tyler I'm sorry. Ryan had several offers from Ivy League schools and has accepted one from Cornell. Avery has the one from Grand Rapids Community College that he's accepted. Jacob had several but he's already announced he plans to keep this commitment to USC." He tapped the letter in front of Jacob and looked at them. "He's the only one that got a full ride without any conditions or stipulations."

Ryan put his hand on Tyler's shoulder. "I know you think yours is from a shit college with all the academic monitoring required... but you could walk on at Grand Rapids, where Avery's going. That's not a bad small school program."

"That's good advice, Tyler." Coach nodded. "You'd get a real chance there to get more experience and show your skill. You could play your way out of there, get more on film for the big schools to look at to make them change their mind about the academics and then could look at transferring to a larger program.”

Tyler's laugh was harsh. “Thanks anyway, but no thanks, coach.” He stood and walked out of the office.

“Let's go guys.” Ryan pushed his chair back and gestured at Jacob and Avery.

“You boys probably should go and talk with Tyler. I don't want him getting upset and doing something foolish.” The coach said as he put the letters back in the folders. “I know your parents also got confirming letters so after you talk with Tyler it's best you go home and discuss with them, too.”

* * *

UTICA EISENHOWER HIGH SCHOOL SENIOR PARKING LOT

They saw him sitting in his Trans Am parked next to Avery's brown Ford Escort that now had its trunk popped open. They got closer and could hear the music and see that he was rolling a joint, his forearms propped on the steering wheel, singing along with the song.

“Are you fucking crazy?” Ryan leaned down to look through the driver side window at him.

Tyler turned the music down but only a little and looked at him without saying anything or stopping twirling paper and weed together.

Avery walked over to his car and shuffled around inside the trunk. He straightened with a pissed off look and came around the Trans Am's passenger side window. He reached in and turned off the stereo. "Hey man, I don't recall telling you that you could get into my stuff!"

The joint was now between Tyler's lips and stuck there as he laughed at Avery's consternation. "I was out..." He picked up the baggie from his lap, sealed it, and tossed to Avery, who caught it and quickly took to his car and re-hid under the spare tire. Tyler's Bic lighter flashed and puffs of pungent smoke billowed around his head.

"I'm not standing here... watching you pull this shit. Tyler, you're a fucking idiot." Jacob was shaking his head and moving toward his car parked next to Ryan's two rows back.

"What are they going to do to me?" Tyler stuck his head out of the car to call to Jacob as he walked away. "Are they going to take away my scholarship—gonna take away our championship?"

With that last comment, Avery muttered something and with a dark look at Tyler he got in his car, seconds later pulling out faster than he should have on school grounds.

Ryan leaned on the left front fender of the Trans Am. "That's pretty shitty, Jennelo. Sometimes you don't give a fuck about your friends, do you?" He felt the car shake as the driver's side door opened and slammed.

"Sometimes, I think my friends don't give a fuck about me." Tyler flicked the stub of the joint—a good size roach—with thumb and forefinger. It arced and landed on the hood of a white Camaro. "I've listened to Jacob talk about USC and to you about going to Cornell— even Avery and how he is going to make the best of it at Grand Rapids." The tendons in Tyler's neck stood out like low-note piano wire.

Ryan stood straight and turned to face him. "If you had taken things, other than football and partying, more seriously you wouldn't be in the situation you're in for college."

His friend's eyes flashed and then muted. "They should take me because I can play." Tyler looked around, his eyes sweeping the cluster of school buildings and the practice field to the left and behind them. "Folks here and around town, they like me because I can play football. Over there..." He cocked his thumb at the field. "I—we—worked our ass off. We sweated and bled. And when we played... we made people happy. Playing's what makes me happiest, too."

Some of that Ryan agreed with but he shook his head. "I think we're at a point where we all have to realize that what's out here..." he mimicked Tyler's scan of their surroundings. "Is just as important or more so than football. After what happened up north, we're fucking lucky to not be in jail." Ryan shook his head again. "I still have trouble sleeping."

"Fuck it." With a last look at the practice field, Tyler slipped his class ring off and Ryan watched as he turned from him and threw it as far as he could.

* * *

TYLER JENNELO'S HOUSE

"That's too bad Tyler. I don't know what to tell you." Rick Jennelo poured a drink and turned to face his son. "I'll pay for you to get into a Division One college somewhere. But I can't pull strings and get you onto their football team."

"You have connections and leverage with lots of backers at different athletic programs. You can get one of them to talk to their head coach and find me a roster spot someplace. Not some bullshit community college." He waved the one offer letter he had received. "I want to play at a college where there's competition and without some bullshit minimum maintained grade requirement." Tyler sat on the edge of his father's desk. "Dad, all I want is a chance to make it on a good team that gets some sports coverage."

"Well, then you should walk on just like your friend Ryan said."

Tyler's face tightened. "So you're not going to help me?"

"I've had to clean up too many of your messes. Because of your temper. Because of your shortsightedness. Because you don't give a damn about anything but having a good time." His dad walked away from him and looked out the window. "The shit that you've pulled, especially what happened at Torch Lake, puts me and my business at risk. I can't tolerate that. If you can't accept things on my terms, then feel free to do things your way on your own."

"Fuck it then." The veins in Tyler's neck stood out. He gripped the corner of the desk like he was going to rip a piece off. "I don't need you. Or your money. That's all you fucking care about anyway so keep it."

Chapter 14

MARCH 1989
TYLER JENNELO

My future beyond graduation didn't have the same certainty as Ryan and Jacob's. Although I had opportunities to play ball at the college level, I fell into a category of prop-48. Lackluster grades and a meager 12 on the ACT would mean I would have to play football at some crappy small college under academic monitoring. With the hopes of raising my grades through a tutorial process. But what if my grades didn't improve? What path would I be left with? A failed existence.

My father was brought up with a strong work ethic and I could still hear him from last night's argument. "Tyler it's time to put glory days behind you and start working while taking some classes at the local community college. That'll give you time to find what you want to do. It's my fault for not pressing you sooner to work that out."

He had a realistic view of life and always had the pulse of the street. The profession he chose dealt with the darker side of life. He was the largest bookmaker in Metropolitan Detroit and ran it all through a small shot and beer joint called The Wolverine on the east side of Detroit.

It wasn't always that way. He started in the late 60s taking mostly smaller action under the flag of the well-known mob boss Joseph Leone. Government crackdowns in the early 80s allowed my father to carve, bit by bit, a piece of the city for himself. Ultimately, with the fall of organized crime in Detroit, my father got control of everything. Government repercussions were harsh but he held firm.

Although it wasn't a respectable line of work like Ryan's or Jacob's father had, he provided for the son he was raising on his own and he had the balls to go out and take what he wanted. I loved him for that.

With what happened up north to Gavin and the investigation weighing heavily on my mind, I decided to take my father's advice and get a job at a mini mall chain health club. I could take some classes and work at a place that would allow me to keep my body solid in the event I wanted to return to the playing field.

My father set up the job and told me I was to report for an interview at the Parkdale Health Spa & Gym. My interview was with the owner, Tom. He was eager to give me a job, most likely to seek favor with my father. Despite that, it was a perfect spot for me to start. I was to clean the club and help the mostly elderly clientele with their workouts. Also, I could make a nice percentage on any new members I brought in the door. The health club was part of a family-owned business with Tom running this particular branch. He didn't spend much time there giving me a lot of latitude for after-hours activities. What a perfect close out to a night of partying with a swim or a long hot tub soak along with a few nonmembers, especially my favorite girls. It was a great way to spend the summer after graduation. Repercussions from what happened at Torch Lake seemed to be fading and only better times were ahead for me.

* * *

AVERY IRONS

Something about what had happened at Torch Lake made me feel that the dreams me and my friends had all our lives might not pan out or go as we had hoped. And if they didn't how was I going to take care of my grandmother? How could I live that life full of all the good things I had dreamed about?

Soon we would all be going in different directions. Jacob to USC in Los Angeles, Ryan to Cornell in Ithaca, New York and I would be going to Grand Rapids. Tyler? I don't know what was going to happen to him. Everything that seemed so sure going into that last playoff game had fallen apart. All because I fumbled the fucking football on the 5-yard line.

I finished smoking the joint and turned down the music. It was too loud for me to think and I needed to figure some things out. Playing football at a small college wasn't what I had counted on. I had grown up always being bigger, faster and stronger than my classmates but that gap had closed the last year or so. What would it be like at the next level?

I remembered the night Tyler's father had taken us to the casino. Yeah, it was illegal, but man was it fun. The food, the drinks, even the girls we weren't supposed to touch but did. But it was the games that really stoked me. I didn't think there was anything but football that could give me such a rush. The $1,000 credit Mr. Jennelo had given me, by the end of the evening, had turned into over $4,000. I was blown away at how I felt as I knew when to bet and when to stay—just some basic Blackjack strategy that Mr. Jennelo had shared with us in the limo ride to the casino. We all knew Ryan was the smartest of us, but somehow sitting there watching the cards turn over on the green felt with the stacks of chips in different colors in front of me, I knew exactly what I was doing with each hand dealt to me. I'd never felt that anywhere but on the football field. Maybe that was my backup plan. To take what seemed to be a knack or gift for Blackjack and use it to make some money.

I remembered what Mr. Jennelo also said in the limo: "I'm proud of you boys and what you've accomplished in sports and the rewards you've achieved and will receive because you are good football players. Football—if you're good or maybe even great—can take you into a professional career. Maybe. Even if it does the odds are that career won't last long. Then what do you have left? That's why you need to focus equally on education, boys. You always have to have a backup plan."

I knew I couldn't go to Mr. Jennelo and pitch him on my plan to get into some low scale, low key, gambling to try it out but Tyler through being around his father knew people that might be able to help me. I grabbed my jacket and headed to where Tyler worked.

* * *

PARKDALE HEALTH SPA & GYM
SHELBY TOWNSHIP

"I can't help you, Avery. My dad is pissed off at me already about what's happened and all the attention and police sniffing around. He'll be even more pissed at me if I help you get sucked into gambling and you lose your ass."

"I just need you to give me the name or introduce me to one of the small places—the ones off your father's radar—just to get a start and see how it goes."

Tyler shook his head again took the towel from around his neck and wiped his face. "I'm sorry Avery."

Avery had thought about that night up north when Tyler had taken something from the body and denied it. "What did you take from Gavin's pocket that night?"

Tyler's face tightened and he was quiet for a moment. "Nothing." He started to turn away from Avery, who grabbed his arm.

"It looked like some kind of key to me. Was it?" He let go of his arm.

"It wasn't anything. Drop it, Avery." Tyler stepped closer and looked down at him.

"Listen," Avery matched his stern look. "You haven't been the same since and it's not just what happened with Gavin. We're all dealing with that. You were worried that only one college offered you a conditional scholarship. In fact, you were pretty pissed off about it. But now you're not. It's like you don't even care about going on to college. What's up, did that key lead you to some--"

Tyler cut him off. "I have a backup plan. Sometimes in the game, you have to adapt and change your scheme... switch your plan."

"Well, I'm in the same situation as you. I need a backup plan and I think I can cut it gambling to make enough money to take care of my grandmother and me. Help me get hooked in." The way Tyler looked at him, he felt he was sitting across from a stranger, not someone he'd spent the last 12 years going to school, growing up and playing football with. "Help me and I won't mention the key again."

"Okay." Tyler's eyes grew darker as they did when he was most intense. "But someday when I need you to stand by me or help... are you gonna be there for me?"

Avery looked up into those dark, glittering, eyes and prayed that that moment would never come. Tyler had changed—hardened—in a way that scared him. He'd always been right on the edge of being too violent, too extreme. Now he seemed way over that line. But he nodded to him anyway. "Sure."

"I know my dad likes you, maybe even more than Ryan and Jacob. Your family situation is more like what he had to go through growing up. But you can't let on that you're gambling. He doesn't want me to get involved—says he has to keep his hands as the only dirty ones in the family—because he wants something better for me. He won't want you getting into it either."

"I won't tell him." Avery relaxed. He was still wary of what Tyler had said, but at least now he had something as a backup plan. "Tyler, there's nothing else I can think of that I can do. I'm not like Jacob or Ryan with their opportunities."

Tyler closed his eyes with a half nod. "We got to do, what we got to do." He opened them but didn't look at Avery. "Right?"

Chapter 15

APRIL 1989
AVERY IRONS

After graduation, my life will be full of holes and it looked like my future would be, too. Grandma had told me, "Avery you have to spend more time on your school work." She'd been holding his report card. "I don't have the book smarts to help you... why don't you ask your friends, maybe that nice Kramer boy?"

But I couldn't do that and now I was paying the price. My poor grades would only allow me to play the game I loved, more than anything, at a small junior college just outside Grand Rapids. I know that a lot of good players, even some that made it to the NFL, went this route and used it as a stepping stone to transfer to a higher quality athletic program at other colleges and major universities. But I couldn't help but feel I was just doing what everyone expected me to do. I looked at it from all angles and could not see it as a way to open doors to the better life I wanted.

The irony was that I was in such a big hurry to move through high school and onto those better things but other than football, I had done nothing to create a structure and foundation to get there. There was so much unknown in my future that scared the hell out of me. I couldn't shake what had happened. That last game where I fumbled, coughing the ball up at the end of the game and lost us our shot at a state championship. I relived that play every night. Thoughts of if only I had made a different spin move or just gone down instead of juking to try and fight for the extra yards and the end zone. Why did this happen? In the 11 games before that one, I'd only had a single fumble. What hurt the most was that I'd let my team down and my three best friends who were like brothers to me.

We had started playing football together when we were just eight years old. From playing in the backyard to Shelby Lions football to junior high and through high school we all had dreamed of playing in the Silverdome for a championship. We had acted it out on grass countless times. We dreamed of it. Each of us telling the others how we would be the one to win it all for them.

Tyler thought he would win the game with an interception and then return it, racing the length of the field through the opposing team, to score the winning touchdown. Ryan's vision was of a weak-side linebacker stunt and breaking through for an explosive hit blindsiding the other team's quarterback to stop their last drive. Of course, Jacob thought he would scramble for the winning touchdown or maybe move around in the pocket his eyes always looking downfield, evading or shedding tacklers, until finding the open receiver for a long touchdown pass. We all thought ours was the most plausible way we would get the victory—our championship.

Instead, my band of brothers watched their dream die. I murdered it with my fumble. Instead, of the guy who had run for 125 yards and two touchdowns, I'll be known forever as the guy who screwed up their perfect season. The guy who lost them their chance to become champions. It broke my heart.

And on that day, the worst day of my life, that's forever etched in my mind something even more terrible and tragic happened. That one fucked up day will haunt my three friends and me for the rest of our days. I closed my eyes and could still feel the bitter cold wind coming off of Torch Lake as I looked down on a body knowing that I had played a part in a man's death. I could still see Gavin's bloody face under the moon and the light from two snowmobiles. What could we have done differently? I know we shouldn't have chased Gavin. But we were so keyed up, all of us still pissed off and angry about the game. We weren't going to back off and let some asshole get away with what he had done in front of our friends.

Maybe we all belonged behind bars. I shook my head and reached for the Crown Royal. The demons were howling and it seemed to help kill the sound of their screams and the pain of remembering that day and night. When it didn't work and the lows got too intense, I hit the powder and it seemed to even me out most of the time. But even then I couldn't shake the hollow feeling inside that ached so terribly. I felt like some manic housewife having a nervous breakdown. I had to keep moving on and let time sort it all out.

When my memories of the past faded away into the present, I focused on keeping up with my routine workouts for the start of summer ball. Why was I doing this? Maybe it was because everyone expected me to fulfill the so-called charmed life we all assumed I would have as we grew older. After I had plowed through my workouts during the day, my only real sense of pleasure came when I made my move to go try my hand at gambling.

Since that night Tyler's dad had picked up the tab for us all at that place he'd taken us, I'd thought over and over again about what I saw there. Men wearing $1,000 suits with sexy, half-dressed, women on each arm and stacks of green cash, money clips thick with it, flashing in and out of their pocket throughout the night. Now, from the moment I got out of the car and stepped inside and heard the action that's when I felt alive. Walking through those doors cleansed me of everything that had happened in the past and I was newborn.

Chapter 16

MAY 1989
RONALD WINSLOW'S OFFICE
SHELBY TOWNSHIP

"I've heard some people talking. I think you should steer clear of those boys."

Jacob Winslow got up and went to stand by his father who was looking out of his window on the sparse off-hour traffic. "Dad, they're my friends. I've known them—you've known them—all my life."

"I know. But still..." he looked up two inches into his son's eyes. "This investigation into what happened with your friends up at Torch Lake is serious. And I didn't want you going on that spring break trip to Cancun with them after that, but I didn't stop you."

"What's got you worried about them?" Jacob felt the clutch of his own concern deep in his gut. Had they talked about that night? He had got punches in on Gavin, too, and had gone all in with Ryan, Avery and Tyler on the cover story. Didn't that make him an accessory? Shit. He shook his head. "What was that, Dad?"

"I said that they've been seen with some questionable people."

"What's that mean?" Jacob's voice sounded angry but was equally worry-tinged.

"I know they're your friends. But they've been seen with some folks on the fringes of dealing drugs and gambling." He sat down in the high-back chair behind his desk. "Tyler and Avery. That's what I heard." He looked up at his son who had so much potential. So much more talent and opportunity. Far more than he had when he was not much older than his boy. He had had a taste of big-time football played in front of 70,000 to 80,000 fans or more and he wanted that desperately for his son. He wanted him to make it all the way through college ball to the pros. He made sure Jacob was paying attention to what he said. "And with that investigation about the man whose body was found after you were up there with your friends, two who apparently fought with him... still going on... you should put some distance between you and them. It happens to high school friends all the time, they go in different directions."

Jacob shook his head but knew he was right. There was too much at stake. "Okay, Dad—okay."

Chapter 17

JUNE 1989
CARLOS HERMOSA'S HEADQUARTERS
DETROIT

Tyler had thought about this—debated it even—for months. What he had taken from Gavin's locker and stuffed in his mattress, still there and untouched, was like a ticking clock the whole time. He listened to it every night as he tried to sleep and it was driving him crazy. Finally, he had to do something. It was time and this was it. He parked a block away and walked up to the backside of the building. He had been there once before, outside, after following Gavin to it. It used to be McCarthy's Bar & Grill on the corner of Jefferson Avenue and Mount Elliot. The building was dilapidated and on the verge of tear-down as part of the Greater Detroit renovation. But it seemed like the city would never get around to that. In the interim it served a purpose. Tyler knew the word on the street was this was where a lot of drugs came in and then moved out onto the streets. He checked the door and was surprised that it opened. But Carlos was reputed to be a badass. Who would fuck with him?

There wasn't anyone around as he walked through to the front part of the building. He heard a voice and saw a young girl, probably the same age as him, come in the main entry. She turned left toward a set of doors he hadn't noticed. He stopped her. "Do you know where I can find Carlos?" She looked him up and down then shrugged, cocking her head at him to follow her.

They went through a storeroom and she still hadn't said a word. She turned right, toward the back of the building Tyler thought, and into a hallway. She stopped at a door that had an opaque glass top-half with faded letters that spelled General Manager on it. She held a hand palm out toward him and then went inside and closed the door in his face. He waited and only a minute later it opened and she crooked an index finger at him to come in.

* * *

Carlos Hermosa waved away the young girl who had walked Tyler Jennelo into his office. "Why are you here kid?"

"Gavin Murdoch mentioned you." Without asking Tyler sat in the single chair in front of the desk.

Carlos slid the handgun from the holster affixed to the underside of his desk. His right thumb found and flipped the safety off. "I don't know anyone by that name."

"I followed him here a couple of times." Tyler sat straighter in the hard wooden chair. "I figured I'd give it a try."

"Give what a try?" Carl's finger tightened on the gun as he drew it onto his lap, pushing his chair back, apparently at ease with Tyler's unexpected appearance and questions.

Tyler looked him in the eye and didn't blink. "I know he worked for you."

"I told you I don't know him." The smile didn't reach his eyes.

"I used to buy from him." Tyler now had a tight grin. "But if you don't know him then I guess it must've been someone else he owes a couple pounds of cocaine and a bag of money to."

Carlos tilted his chair forward, pulled the gun out and leveled it at Tyler's face. Tyler's eyes widened over the front sight of his gun but again didn't blink. "You want to think about what you're saying. And maybe keep that mouth shut."

"I have it. The cash and the coke." Tyler didn't move.

"You interest me, kid." Carlos set the gun down on his desk the muzzle still pointed at Tyler. "What do you want?"

"I want a job."

"What's your name?"

"Tyler Jennelo."

"I know that last name from somewhere. A numbers guy—sports betting—I'm thinking. He your father? He sure ain't going to like you being here around me. Some of the people he's connected to... well, they don't get along with some of the people I work for." He spun the handgun on his desk until the muzzle pointed at Tyler. "Why should I trust you?"

"Fuck my father. I'm on my own. I can only count on me now." Tyler's grin broadened. "Just think how bent out of shape those guys you mentioned, that your people don't like, are going to be when they find out I'm working for you. They'll think I know something and you've got me spilling my guts."

Carlos looked thoughtful. "Do you..." He spun the gun again and kept it twirling on the desk. "Do you know anything that might be helpful to me?"

Tyler thought of all that had happened. No football. His friends, what he thought were his friends, pulling away from him.

Sure, the thing at Torch Lake had mostly been his fault but still they'd all agreed, one for all and all for one. Yeah. It didn't seem like that anymore. They'd all still go off to fulfill their future plans and leave him behind. He focused on Carlos. "I could tell you yes or maybe... but I don't play games like that. No, I don't know anything about my father's business dealings or details on who it's with. But they're still going to squirm second-guessing whether I'm telling you anything important. So you can watch that happen. I'll work for you in distribution or collections; it doesn't matter. I just want to make real money and have fun. Fuck everyone else."

The spinning gun stopped pointed at the wall. "Like I said, you're interesting; you got balls to come in here like this. Your dad's not going to like you working for me. But we'll give it a try. It seems I've got an opening. Let's see if you fill it."

* * *

EARLY JULY 1989
ANTRIM COUNTY SHERIFF'S OFFICE (TORCH LAKE AREA)

The homicide detective picked up the phone and dialed the Shelby Charter Township Police Department. "Detective Sgt. Larkin, please. Thanks."

He looked over his notes and shook his head. It had been months. There was something underneath the four boys' story but he couldn't dig it out. He heard someone pick up the line at the other end. "Hello? Right, this is Lieutenant Horton up at the Antrim County Sheriff's office. I just wanted to update you. Based on what we've seen and after interviewing the boys I agree with you. The coroner's report clearly shows massive head trauma as the cause of death but there's nothing to tie it to the boys. There's something suspicious but no evidence to prove anything or to even merit pushing harder on this to break their story. Right. I know given who the victim is... or was... no one's going stir anything up if it goes cold. And that girl, Kelly, she's pretty sketchy, too. Her accusations and suspicions just aren't backed by evidence and that Kramer kid's lawyer uncle is constantly up our ass on this. I'm going to call him and the kid's parents to tell them their sons are no longer suspects. But just to close the loop on record I suspect that something did happen up here with those four boys and this Gavin Murdoch; more than they've admitted. No. I don't think the Winslow kid was too deeply involved. For chrissake he's going to USC on a full football scholarship—no way he's involved with something that would jeopardize that. Likewise, with that Kramer kid going to Cornell. The Irons kid—maybe but I don't think he's the guy. My money is on Tyler Jennelo—if he hasn't done it already, that kid is going to snap and kill someone one day... He's got that look in his eyes. Yeah, you've seen it before, too. But as things stand right now; no evidence. Yeah, right."

He hung up the phone and studied his notes for a while and then shaking his head stacked them neatly and put back in the folder. He passed the Active—In Progress filing cabinet and carried it to the one in the corner. The light layer of dust on top was disturbed when he set the folder on top as he unlocked the 4th drawer down, marked M—P, and put the folder in it. He closed it and relocked the cabinet.

Back at his desk, he took out the contact sheet with the boy's names and their parents. With a sigh, he picked up the phone and started dialing.

Chapter 18

JULY 1989
TYLER JENNELO'S HOUSE

TYLER JENNELO

Gavin had handled distribution and collections but he wasn't much on bringing in new sales for Carlos. But I knew tons of guys who used marijuana, or as we called it, Janie, as part of their party experience. It would be so easy to connect with guys from school, past graduates, friends from surrounding areas and guys I knew who used to be on sports teams I played with or against. And even my new job working at the spa was a perfect cover for me. I would meet a steady flow of people that might become customers. One thing was for sure, it was in high demand and nobody would suspect a guy—a former football star—like me to be selling dope. I was hesitant but had decided I wanted to move forward and that's why I met with Carlos.

A routine was quickly established. Once a week one of Carlos's men, who had become a spa member, would come in but not to work out or enjoy the amenities. He would take my keys and go to my car, parked in back of the building where it was unlikely to be seen, and load the trunk of my yellow Trans Am full of product.

At first, I was unsure of the quantity, what was needed, and what I could expect to make from it. That first time I had asked Carlos's man about what he had just delivered for me to distribute.

The man shrugged his shoulders, "It's been the same quantity for maybe a year... Carlos wasn't too happy that this area wasn't developing. I don't know what kind of cut Gavin was getting but I think he was raking $4,000 to $5,000, maybe less or a bit more, for himself every couple weeks."

I took a deep breath when I heard that. So much for starting out small. Maybe this was just my way of getting back at my dad and showing him I didn't need him to make something of myself. Maybe I just wanted something to occupy my mind. I thought of Ryan, Avery, and Jacob. We'd been like ghosts that last half of our senior year. I think people figured it was because of losing the Catholic Central game—and maybe that was part of it—but it was all about what happened up north and what we had done. What I had done. What I had dragged all my friends into covering up. I shook my head to clear it. It didn't matter anymore.

Even though Carlos's man seemed to think it wasn't that much... it was a lot of money to me. My new venture was on fast wheels and that extra income was going to provide for one hell of a summer. Working at the spa, flying under the radar, and selling some weed and cocaine was pretty simple. Making that kind of money on my own did take my mind off of how I felt about what had happened in the past and the falling out with my father. Maybe at some point, he would understand what I was doing and why. After all, he had chosen an illegal way to make a living. But drugs carry a different label than bookmaking and gambling; that profession and particular vice got a lot of tacit approval and had an established routine from some authorities of looking the other way. I knew I would have to be careful.

That first delivery day from Carlos, after work, I rushed home and pulled my car in and closed the garage door behind me. I wanted to evaluate the new inventory. I had five pounds of marijuana and a half a pound of cocaine. I decided then that I didn't want to get involved with direct selling to users like Gavin had—though I still had a commitment to Carlos to supply them—instead my plan was to find five guys willing to take small amounts of inventory and then have them sell it for me. Also, I figured breaking it up and selling it in smaller quantities would have a higher yield and more profit, which was a very attractive side benefit. So if I could find five solid, reliable, guys as my initial sales force, they could deal with the end consumer and there would be less risk to me. Besides, I didn't want some punk calling me day and night for a quarter ounce or a gram to get him by.

I kept a low profile within my tight group. My old friends knew something was going on, but I never told them any details or specifics. They didn't need to know. They had their own things that they were doing for their future and so was I. Since graduation and over the summer I'd seen less of them.

* * *

JULY 1989

THE UNIVERSITY OF SOUTHERN CALIFORNIA CAMPUS

JACOB WINSLOW

I can still hear my father talking. "Jacob, it happens to high school friends all the time; they go in different directions." But he didn't know—hopefully never would know—what had really happened at Torch Lake.

But I don't know that even distancing myself from them and moving to Los Angeles would change how I felt. The horrible event that took place up north still wakes me up most nights. The investigation that followed it, though the police say the case has grown cold, still leaves doubt in my mind if I will ever completely believe we are in the clear. My dreams suggest I'll most likely be handcuffed to this thing the rest of my life.

Only one thing has provided some relief from our actions and that is time. Months removed from our terrible mistake and the likelihood of criminal charges have diminished. All I want to do is stay off anyone's radar, work out and keep throwing. It'll be a new start. A chance to put this behind me and focus on one thing. Football and to become the starting quarterback at USC.

I've never been in better shape in my life. My workouts put me in a different place and I was already 40 seconds under my six-minute mile time. I had dabbled in a cycle of the steroid called Anadrol with Ryan and it sure made a difference in my strength. I went from throwing 70 yards to 85 inside of two months. What was more important was I could throw a frozen rope on any 35 to 45 yard out pattern. Even though Mike Churchill will be the starter with two years under his belt, I think I'm ready to compete with anyone. My goal was to be ready to play immediately. When and if I get my chance I will seize the moment and make everyone proud. USC is filled with a rich football tradition especially at the quarterback position and I'm ready to be part of it.

I knew, from all the letters and offers I received from colleges and recruiters that called on me, that USC was the place for me. My first visit back in the spring had made it my solid choice. The campus is fairly small but its confines reflect a true feeling of LA living. The school was filled with well-taken care of blonde women. At home, for every three nice looking girls it seemed that there were seven that weren't. At USC, the ratio was switched and at a minimum was 7 to 3. Maybe the weather was the reason for this difference. California didn't offer co-eds the chance to wear extra layers of clothes to cover the extra layers of skin added on during the winter months. What you gained is what you showed.

My new home for at least the next four years was an oasis. I shared an apartment with another incoming freshman football player, a tight-end from Houston, Texas. His name was Zach Torrence and based on our first encounter I knew we would be compatible. The apartment was conveniently located and our neighbors were three sophomore females from Palm Springs. They seemed very willing to provide us with the full Southern California experience. Judging from the conversations with the older players it was apparent why none of them wanted to graduate.

Following my acceptance of a full ride scholarship to play for the Trojans, after graduation I received a first-class ticket and package labeled, a *Gift from the Gods*. The itinerary explained how it was a chance to meet the players and, more importantly, my new roommate. I figured the title of the package for some Greek mythological theme based on tradition. In reality, it was a party set up by the Delta Omega fraternity better known as the 'Football House.' It was a tradition like none other. Upon entering the frat house, we were welcomed by a long-bearded, elderly, man dressed in ancient Greek fashion. "The gods have bestowed favor upon you." He smiled at us. "Trojan warriors indulge…" He backed away spreading his arms wide to invite us in. There were five females behind the bar and many others waiting to engage in conversation. I became acquainted with two graduate students named Nikki and Jennifer. I had my doubts as to their enrollment in the school but had a strong belief that their higher education would pay them large dividends in the future. My recollection of the evening was perfectly described by the words Zach, my new roommate, whispered in my ear a few minutes after we got there. "I think we chose the right school."

Time could not move fast enough to make this my new home and put the past behind me. Summer had cruised by and my contact with my three best friends was minimal. We had occasionally gone out together, but it was easy to see the four of us were on different paths. I saw Ryan the most, working out at the gym, but our conversations were strictly based on future plans. Tyler was wrapped up in the party scene and the only time I would see him would be at a bar or sometimes at one of his frequent after-hours sessions at his health club. As for Avery, he was in his own world and had basically withdrawn from everything and everyone. I knew he had gotten into gambling pretty heavy and that was something I didn't have much interest in. Staying up all night playing Blackjack and too much partying was a recipe for poor physical performance. I wasn't going to jeopardize my chance at USC. I had to keep my distance from anything that would be detrimental to my goals.

But now that I was here all the excitement to get the hell out of Dodge was still diminished by a certain sadness. I thought that no matter what, my new teammates at USC all from different parts of the country would never equal the three friends I had back in my hometown. We had grown up together, played football all our lives together and gone to battle every Friday night for years. Once I got off that plane to come here, to USC, nothing would ever be the same again. I had left so many things behind. But time couldn't be stopped and I had to move forward and hopefully could forget that one horrible night at Torch Lake.

* * *

JULY 1989
RYAN KRAMER'S HOUSE

It felt odd to be doing it. Ryan was packing his winter clothes knowing he'd need them in Ithaca, New York, too. He sat on the edge of his bed and thought about how his world had changed in less than a year. After what happened at Torch Lake they had gone through the rest of high school in a haze. Their once tightknit group stayed together but it felt as if they were just going through the motions. Even during their spring break trip to Cancun, it was if they were ghosts, shells of former friends, just getting hammered and passing the time.

Avery seemed to have been hit the worst and overindulged in everything. He had never been the same since that night at the lake. He lived on Crown Royal and for the almost endless trips to the small gambling halls with girls he picked up. Ryan didn't know how he managed the back and forth driving or what he had used for money to gamble. But Ryan knew Mr. Jennelo wouldn't be happy if he found out.

Tyler had something going on and Ryan hardly saw him anymore and when he did he wouldn't talk about what he was up to.

Ryan knew that the highs they had felt on the football field just weren't found off it. Both Avery and Tyler desperately needed that kind of high. The kind they manufactured outside the game were a poor substitute. Guilt and regret don't go away while nursing a major hangover or riding a winning streak; they just get numbed. No matter how many of them you string together.

Jacob was flying as straight as an arrow. He was locked in on his target, already at USC, and he would not miss.

And Amanda? She didn't seem to want to have anything to do with him. Ryan Kramer was persona non grata. It looked like he would never get another chance with her and that, more than anything, made him feel like nothing he did now or in the future would ever matter again. Now that the investigation into them and Torch Lake had been dropped he needed to move on too. He was glad he would be leaving for Cornell soon.

* * *

JULY 1989
DETROIT, CASS AVENUE AND 3RD STREET
BEHIND CHUNG'S CHINESE RESTAURANT

AVERY IRONS

The names that Tyler gave me had led to a series of adventures in learning. He had warned me, "Avery, some of these guys are rough—they're not going to care about anything but what money you leave with them when you walk away. Watch your back."

None of the venues, certainly not this one, were anything close to the place that Mr. Jennelo had taken us to that night we won our final game to end the regular season undefeated. Most of them were just storefronts with the gambling done in the back without fanfare, furnishings or the flare of what I still remembered from that night. But I treated each one like the practice fields they were. I sensed that I had a good head for cards; the basic strategy of when to stand, hit, split and double-down came easily to me. It was just like picking the right time to make a cut, to hit the right hole and explode through.

I had roughly $90,000, most of it was what my grandmother had set aside for me for college. But I had added to it through work and saving birthday and Christmas money over the years. I had learned about hard work from my father. He had worked the night shift at Chrysler so I didn't see him much but on his days off. When I was young, we would play catch in the backyard. He was a warm man, always optimistic despite having to carry the burden of my alcoholic mother. But he had died of an aneurysm when I was in fourth grade.

After my father had died, my mother had wasted little time in getting remarried. Maybe it was her fear of being alone or the need to make someone else miserable. Her new husband had spent most of his time on his stupid hobbies and had no interest in athletics or sports. But sports, especially football, became my life. Needless to say, my family life, though tolerable, was strained. It got better when I moved in with my grandmother and it was she who really raised me. Now I didn't have anything I thought I would have when I graduated from high school. I had dreamed of a scholarship to play at a big university—the big stage and maybe beyond to the NFL. Instead, all I had to look forward to was barely a chance to play the game I loved most at a junior college level. It wasn't what I dreamed of.

I shook all those thoughts off. I needed to get my head into my game when I approached the table. Blackjack was the game that gave me instant gratification. I had started small, which was okay at first. Then I began to notice the thrill of winning $500 was fading. It wasn't enough to pull me away from reality. So I did what most addicts would do when they needed more of a thrill. I pushed my betting higher. I looked for the floor boss. "I want to raise the table stakes." I fanned the bills in my hand and saw the light in his eyes.

"I think we can accommodate you." The man grinned, waving me toward a back room reserved for special visitors to his den.

That night I won big. I walked away from the tables with an extra $30,000 in my pocket. Drunk on all the free bourbon they'd plied me with and still on a gambler's high, I took one of the banded, strapped, stacks, and put in an envelope. I popped the trunk of my Escort open—if things kept going like this, I had plans to buy a new Corvette—and lifted my spare to the reveal the dirt and grease covered, shallow tin box I kept my stash in. I put the stack in thinking, here's something for a rainy day. I'd not felt this good since that win over Lake Orion.

The next several nights it was if I had pissed off all the gambling gods. The cards were against me and I was down $75,000. All I had left from my original bankroll was $45,000 and that included the emergency stash.

After a few days of being swallowed by self-pity and short fused outbursts, I felt the need to come to grips with reality. I needed to put myself back together and change my ways. Forget about my losses with the belief it will all work itself out. Be positive and move into a better space. For two weeks I pushed my workouts to the highest levels. No ingestion of alcohol or mind altering drugs. I was feeling better about myself and felt like I could suppress my misfortunes. Block them out and keep only positive thoughts flowing through my mind. A hard thing to do, training your mind to eliminate so many horrible events. Mental trickery that I thought I was beginning to master to ease my bewildered soul. In a couple of days, I was to report for the start of football at Grand Rapids Community College. I was going to be tested on all of my physical abilities. The three big ones: bench press and times in the 40 and mile and a half run. My numbers were excellent with my bench press at 350lbs, a 4.4 sec 40 time and an 8-minute 30-second mile and a half. Not bad for letting myself go for half the summer. My workout routines were putting me into great shape for the season.

But my anxious desire to return to the gambling halls, which had become my new home, grew and grew. Finally, I had to return to that routine, too. That night I went back to the tables. Bad move. I left that night having lost everything and still owed money. I didn't know what the fuck I was going to do.

Chapter 19

LATE JULY 1989
AMANDA'S APARTMENT AT MOUND AND 24-MILE ROAD

"She doesn't want to see you, Tyler." Amanda told him for the third time and kept her foot planted firmly behind the half-open door. "And don't go to her work. The manager there is going to call the cops the next time you show up there."

"Please, just for a few minutes." His right hand curled around the edge of the door and she knew he was going to push. She hefted the ashtray she picked up when she saw it was him through the peephole. "Shit!" He pulled his hand back when she cracked him across the fingers with it. "Dammit, Amanda!"

His eyes were wide and pupils dilated. She knew he was high on something. "Just because you suddenly have all this cash to throw around doesn't make up for you hitting her."

Tyler brought his face closer to the door opening. "That was an accident. She shouldn't have tried to grab my arm. I didn't mean to elbow her in the face." He gritted his teeth as the words came out like he had said them a dozen times before and was tired of repeating them. "Even the police chalked it up as an accident."

"Yeah." Amanda was ready to slam the door on him. "Because she didn't press charges and neither did that guy you started the fight with."

"I didn't start anything," Tyler muttered and dropped his eyes. He stepped back into the hallway outside the apartment door. "I just want to see her. I'm gonna be moving downtown... I want to tell her I'm sorry before I go."

"Say it then."

Amanda looked over her shoulder. Shelley was standing there with an old blanket that had a rainbow design that arced from end-to-end draped over her shoulders covering the front of her pajamas. She looked at him with her right eye since the left was swollen shut. The EMT's bandage was still in place, sealing the large cut under the eye. The bruising around it had spread down her cheek and across her swollen nose. Stiffening her stance, Amanda heard Tyler as he moved closer to the door again. He kept his hand away from it this time but leaned forward.

"I'm so sorry, baby... Let me--" His eyes stared past Amanda.

Shelley cut him off. "Say it 1,000 times more and it still won't matter." She stepped closer but was still behind Amanda and to one side. "Don't you get it, Tyler? It's not the words that come out of your mouth. It's how you act. How you treat people." She paused and the tears coursing down her cheek threatened to loosen the bandage under her eye. "It's how you treat me." She turned away.

Amanda closed and locked the door. She stood there with back against it. She knew he was still on the other side of the door. Then the feeling of someone shifting from foot to foot inches away, and the sound of their breathing stopped. He was gone.

She checked the door one more time and then went to the little kitchen and picked up the phone and looked at the dial pad. She had thought about it a thousand times. This time, she had to call him. She punched the numbers.

"Ryan? Hi, it's... oh. It's been a while and I thought you wouldn't... I'm fine. How are you? I know it's getting close to time for you to leave. Oh, tomorrow... really? Maybe. I don't know, Ryan, maybe before you go." She leaned her head against the cool metal of the refrigerator. "I know. Listen, I'm calling you because Tyler was just here. Have you seen him lately? No, me neither until just now. I know he's seen Shelley a few times. That's why he was here. You heard about him hitting here. Well, he did; it was kind of an accident during a fight she was trying to break up. Yeah. But hey, he was kind of scary. It was like a Jack Nicholson in *The Shining* moment. Yeah, the one that scared the crap out of me. Tyler was at our door trying to get in to see Shelley. No. I stopped him; I blocked the door. I'm okay. Really, I'm okay. But can you talk to him? Tell him not to do that ever again. He said he's moving to Detroit. I wish it were farther away." She had walked as far as the cord would let her and moved back. "Just tell him to leave Shelley alone. Okay? Thanks. What's that? No, Ryan. I don't know. Maybe before you go." She hung up the phone and cried.

* * *

PARKDALE HEALTH SPA & GYM

He watched as Tyler sprayed the exercise bench with disinfectant and then wiped it down.

"I thought you were running the place and had people to do that for you?" Ryan laughed. At the look on Tyler's face, he added, "Just kidding you, man."

"What do you need Ryan?" Tyler didn't look happy to see him.

"I haven't seen you around much since graduation."

"Cause I haven't been around much." Tyler tossed the rag he'd used in the laundry bin.

"Yeah, over in the city mostly." Ryan paused. "A lot with your new friends." Ryan sat on the bench Tyler had just cleaned. "Amanda told me you're moving there, into the city."

"You sound like you'll miss me." Tyler strode to the front door and locked it. "I'm closing up so you'll have to leave out the back with me."

"I do miss you and so does Avery and Jacob."

"Really?" Tyler gave him a look. "Jacob, too? I bet he misses me." He laughed as he secured the office door and shut off the front lights. "I figured Jacob was too busy California dreaming. Did he say anything to you before he left? I sure didn't see him."

"We're all still friends, Tyler." Ryan followed him through the storeroom to the back. "Aren't we?" He watched as he got out his keys. "Amanda says you scared her trying to see Shelley." He reached over to tap him on the arm when he didn't look at him. "Hey, it's probably best if you leave Shelley alone, Tyler. Let her go. Don't go around her and Amanda again."

He still didn't look up as he found the right one on his key ring. Before he opened the rear exit, he turned on him. Ryan saw the anger spread across Tyler's face.

"You know, I thought after what happened—when everything had died down—that it would all go back to the way it was before. Even with losing that last fucking playoff game we'd still move forward with what we all dreamed about. But it hasn't. Nothing's the same." Tyler unlocked the door, opened it and they stepped out into a still warm night. Heat lightning illuminated the summer sky as he locked the door behind them. "And..." He looked back at Ryan as he walked to his car. "It never will be again." He got into his car started it and shifted to back the car to where it pointed down the access between the buildings and the fence separating the residential development from the strip mall.

Ryan raised his hand to stop Tyler as he pulled forward. "With Torch Lake behind us, we can all still realize our dreams or maybe something close enough."

Tyler's bitter laugh made him doubt his own words. "Yeah, maybe for golden boy Jacob and you, I hear you're leaving tomorrow for Cornell... and Avery, I got some doubts there. Keep dreaming, Ryan." He scoffed not looking at him.

"What about you?" Ryan bent down to look at Tyler eye to eye through the car window.

"Me... I'm gonna do what I gotta do." The tires squealed as he peeled out.

Ryan straightened and started the long walk around the row of buildings to the front lot where he'd parked his car. As he walked, it churned around in his head. It was time for him to get out of Michigan and put everything and everyone behind him.

Chapter 20

AUGUST 1989

TYLER JENNELO

The five guys I selected to work with were stoners and casual users I knew that had some street sense, too. One was a year behind me in school; one I graduated with who was on a co-op plan with General Motors. He had a full scholarship to GMI and was a very smart guy. The others were in colleges that had a large pool of students to peddle their products. They were former football players I knew I could trust once I reconnected with them. Once the fall term started in a month, they would come into town to meet with me long enough to stock up and then go back to their college dorms.

For the local guys, 90% of the distribution took place at a nearby shopping mall called Lakeside. Not in the crowded parking lots as one might expect, but inside at what was often the busiest part of the mall. I would put the product in a Hudson's shopping bag with a few shirts over the top. The associate of the moment was instructed to bring the same size Hudson's department store bag with a few shirts covering the buy money. Our encounter would usually consist of a slice of pizza and an inconspicuous exchange of bags as we rose from the food court table and exited the mall.

It was too easy and gave me a rush I hadn't felt since game day on the football field. I would never have to touch the product other than when I would pull some buds from the tight bundle I received from Carlos's man, for my personal use. I would hook up with my college sellers at their houses when they would return from school about every two weeks. The demand on the campuses was really climbing.

After only one month and a couple of transactions, my college guys wanted to bump their quantity to three pounds every two weeks. I guess there were a lot of pow-wows and heavy thinkers at their academic institutions that needed a little chemical enhancement. I was now pushing 15 pounds of Carlos's grass and a pound of coke every two weeks. I was making nine grand every shipment.

I sold my Trans Am and bought a Caprice Classic Brougham because I sure needed the trunk space. The money was pouring in and I was amazed how that happened in such a short period of time. My new enterprise was clean, precise and so easy to operate. But even so it had helped to keep my mind off of what had happened with Gavin at Torch Lake. With the call our parent's had received from Lieutenant Horton that we were no longer suspects, it meant an ever more fading possibility of getting caught and going to jail. After all these months I still thought that bastard Gavin got what he deserved. His death had sure created an opportunity for me with Carlos, but deep down I still carried the guilt that my friends had paid a price for my anger. Whenever I found myself thinking that I shook it off. For now, all I wanted to do was to have a great time.

My biggest problem was where to stash all the cash I was making. Before long for every pound of inventory I got rid of I would make 1,000% profit. That translated into $18,000 a month in my pocket tax-free. I was 18 years old and had more money than I could spend. I opened five different checking accounts at local banks in some of the surrounding small towns and bought tons of clothing and jewelry to spread things out. At night, during bar time with my new friends, let's just say nobody ever paid for a drink. I quickly became one of Carlos's best distributors and collectors. He took notice and invited me to visit him at his posh house on Orchard Lake. He frequently made trips to Cancun and invited me along to check out other areas of his operations.

By then I didn't have a regard for anyone or anything other than living the high life. No self-indulgent expense was out of reach and I made sure to capture and experience them all. Late nights at the bars, and closing out the evening with groups of girls back at the health club. It was an 18-year-old boy's wet dream and I was living it. I drifted further apart from Ryan, Avery, and Jacob. They all had gone on with their plans for college and things that took them away from Shelby—but I was gonna be the one to have the last laugh. I'd make more money than any of them and have more fun. They might go to college, but my education from the street would exceed theirs from in the classroom.

Chapter 21

AUGUST 1989
SHELBY TOWNSHIP

"Oh, remember this... I love it!" Shelley turned up the volume. Richard Marx's voice delivered memories Amanda would rather forget. "All at once I looked and you were gone," she sang along.

Amanda reached for the knob cranking it down. "Yeah, I do remember it."

"Oh..." Shelley knew what she meant. "Have you heard from Ryan lately?" Taking one hand off the steering well, she patted Amanda's arm.

"No," She shook her head and looked out the window at the town—the scenery—she'd seen virtually every day of her life. Even turned down she could still hear the song and that line. Only for her, she was still where she was when she and Ryan had made plans to leave. Instead of going to college or leaving for a new job and life in Detroit or Chicago she was staying where everything was always the same, in her hometown. She sighed. "I saw his mom at the bank the other day. She said Ryan was settled in at Cornell."

"Did you get his phone number?"

"Why would I need it?" She looked at Shelley.

Shelley gave her that, don't screw around you know why, look back. She had used it countless times that summer trying to get her to call Ryan.

"I don't need to call Ryan. He seemed in kind of a rush to go and was in such a hurry he didn't even call me before he left." She felt guilty at the lie. He had tried to see her and she'd put him off until it was too late and he had to leave. She unbuckled her seatbelt as Shelley pulled into the care center parking lot. She opened the door and got out. "Thanks for the ride this morning."

"Hey!" Shelley called to her and Amanda leaned down to look through the passenger side window at her. "Do you need me to pick you up this evening?"

"No thanks. My mom will be here to visit dad and I'll go home with her." She straightened and walked quickly to the employee entrance. Turning the knob, she pasted a dutiful smile on her face as she stepped inside. She should be thankful she was able to find this job to help her mother. She'd never have been able to afford her father's care since his dementia diagnosis if it wasn't for her discount and the money that she contributed each month. And she got to see that he received attention and care that they normally didn't give the residents. But it was only on rare moments that he realized she was his daughter. Mostly he only knew her by her name tag.

As she punched in she thought of them all: Shelley still waitressing, Tyler deeply into drugs and dealing by all she'd heard but no one saw too much of him around Shelby anymore—mostly he was in Detroit. No one had seen or heard from Avery in weeks. Jacob was off in Los Angeles but she'd seen him for a little while before he left. And Ryan, oh, Ryan. She softly sang that line from the song that hurt so much. She realized that she had let it become a reality in what had happened to them, "All at once I looked and you were gone."

She opened the door to her father's room. "Good morning Dad."

He looked up puzzled and she saw his eyes go to her badge. "Good morning... Amanda?"

Chapter 22

SEPTEMBER 1989
GRAND RAPIDS COMMUNITY COLLEGE
GRAND RAPIDS, MICHIGAN

"I need your help." The young man at the pay phone kept his back to the other students passing down the hallway near him. He took another pill and dry swallowed it, something he'd learned to do easily. The pain in his shoulder wouldn't let up. You get hit a lot harder at the next level and the practices and games had been punishing. The man on the other end of the line answered him and he could hear the hard edge in his voice.

"I've done all I can for you."

"Please, I've always been able to count on you."

The quiet hiss on the line stopped with his voice. "I've helped you plenty, Avery." The static hiss returned. "When I found out you were in deep with small-timers that'll cut you up to collect their money I've covered you when you got overextended. But I can't keep doing it."

The line hissed again. The man on the other end didn't say anything. "I have to make some money… I can't tell her about what I've lost." Now his desperateness was evident. He'd blown most of what his grandmother had given him on gambling and Darvocet he had been buying from the team's trainer just so he could get through practice and his drives to and from his gambling outings in Detroit and school. He rubbed his eyes. It was all running together and hard to keep his mind straight. The only time it felt clear was at the tables with a drink in his hand and a pocket full of pills he'd pop all night like they were M&Ms.

"You need to focus on school and football. Gambling... yes, some people make their living from it but for most people it's a dead end. I can't give you any money—you're into me too much for that but I'll tell someone I know you want to upgrade your activities. You'll need some front money, but he'll match it to give you leverage and then no more help from me... I can't help you if you don't get off the booze and pills." The line went dead.

"You done yet?" The kid poked him gesturing at the phone.

Avery put it back in the cradle. "Yeah. I'm done."

After Rick Jennelo had hung up, he dialed a new number. It answered. "I need to talk to Frank."

* * *

The building was an old downtown mansion that had been joined with a couple of surrounding buildings into almost an enclave for illegal gambling in the Detroit area. Avery looked around and smiled. He remembered the night Mr. Jennelo had brought them here. It was the Taj Mahal of gambling in Detroit. Not like the series of gambling halls and smaller, less opulent, casinos he'd had successes and recent failures in. He didn't dwell on the losses. His money trouble was already forgotten though he was riding along on a line of credit without a net.

A man met him at the door. "I'm Frank and I understand you're a new high-roller and we're to give you the VIP treatment." He scanned Avery from head to toe.

Avery couldn't tell if his smile was sincere or condescending. He decided the former. "The gentleman who recommended me must believe so." He breathed in the air; the atmosphere. He felt he was where he was supposed to be and everything would be fine. He'd win and win big and everything would work out.

Frank's smile glinted like a knife cutting meat under a bright dining table light. "Welcome, Mr. Irons."

He gave Avery a complete rundown of all the amenities, enjoyment and entertainment and games of chance he was about to encounter. Avery's eyes kept coming back to the Blackjack tables. Especially the one he had won big at that first night with Mr. Jennelo's reward for the unbeaten regular season.

"I'll show you your room so you can drop your bag." Frank gestured for him to follow as he moved toward the main stairway.

Two hours later, Avery had already eaten dinner in the luxury suite he had been comped. He had taken another Darvocet and some speed—to keep him sharp—and was back downstairs and in the middle of making a run at the tables. The main floor was almost a cathedral setting. Unlike the movies he had seen of gambling in Las Vegas, which is a more raucous setting, this was quieter but just as intense. Maybe even more so. Sitting in his chair and the table he'd played at the one time before, he was up $5,000. That feeling of belonging had certainly settled firmly in his bones. A girl brought his drinks and on the silver platter, either side of the glass, were four long lines and a rolled up $100 bill. He took the drink in one gulp and then the lines in what seemed a steady snort. He wiped the residue from the bill licking his fingers and handed it to the girl. "This is for you."

Her nipples peeked at him as she bent over him almost brushing them on his fingertips. "Thank you, sir. I look forward to serving you."

Chapter 23

SEPTEMBER 1989
CASINO - FRANK'S PLACE
DOWNTOWN DETROIT

AVERY IRONS

From the moment Frank said, "Have a good time, Avery," and had left me at my favorite table things had gone well. Drink after drink the cards kept coming my way. It felt like something or someone had a hand in delivering them to me to scrape and strip away the memories that tortured me. I'd had five straight weekends of winning and turned that into a nice bankroll. I still needed to share some sort of joy with anyone that could take me to another place. There were girls just for that purpose. Renée, Teresa, Kelly, Jenny, Samantha, or Mia. I knew little about them personally; only what they looked like on the outside. Maybe inside they too were dodging the reality of their own life in some way.

My luck continued and the ultimate gamblers high came on a Saturday evening after a Detroit Tigers game. I sat down, completely wasted on my usual mix of Crown Royal and cocaine, and turned $10,000 into $100,000. It was the best day I ever had at the tables. Frank, my gambling host, congratulated me. I felt great and followed him to the bar. "I think I need to celebrate." Frank smiled at me, nodded and sat down next to a man at the bar who motioned for me to join them.

The man sitting next to Frank was older and had a weathered face and hands to match. He held one of them out and as I shook his hand, it felt like leather. "My name's Carpenter Dave," he smiled, accustom to how odd his name sounded. "Frank here tells me you're quite the gambler... a real up and comer." He looked out over the house tables and the dozens of people busy with their vice. "Did you bet on that Tigers game?"

I looked at Frank and knew that he had made some big scores in sports betting through Tyler's father. It was like lightning struck me right at that instant. Why not take my good fortune and my winnings with this hot streak and parlay it into the big-time? I looked around me. This is where I belonged. The wad of money, all $100,000, was burning a hole in my pocket to do something with it. Why not? I sat down next to Frank, who leaned back so I could see past him to Carpenter Dave. "No I didn't but maybe I should have." I didn't know if he was connected in some way to Mr. Jennelo but I wanted to learn how to get in on the action. Tyler's father controlled most of Metro Detroit gambling and he had given me access to the table games here by way of Frank's good graces and a credit line. But I didn't want him to know how deep I was in, and I wanted to up the stakes. Because then he would try to sit me down and give me the big brother or father talk—he'd already cautioned me to keep it small and under control. And I didn't want that. I needed real action. Big-time action. "How do I go about getting in on that, you know, betting on professional sports?" I looked across Frank at Carpenter Dave.

He nodded at me with a slow smile. "I have some resources and can get you into anything, and I mean anything, that you want."

* * *

Frank and Carpenter Dave were one-stop shopping for all my needs. A quick call to them for my picks and supplies was the center point of my day. I showed up in the evening and enjoyed a comped room including female companionship and a credit line for the tables. It was a systematic schedule and my sports betting focused on baseball. My theory which had some success, at first, was to bet on the better pitcher in the game and that should yield the greatest victories. Unfortunately, I never paid much attention to how good the closer was.

Then the vehicle carrying all my luck started to leak oil in a big way. Not long after I started betting on baseball and heavily at the Blackjack tables my streak faded and things went south. I staggered up to my suite as the closer of the team I was betting on would give up three runs in the ninth. I would lose my ass on that game. I had lost favor with the gambling gods and their vengeance rained down on me. I took a few days off to get over my latest setbacks.

Every morning I woke up with a horrible feeling in the pit of my stomach not knowing why. Was it because of my new label as the guy who choked in the most important football game in his once promising career? Was it what happened at Torch Lake and I expected some kind of punishment for helping to cover up Gavin's murder? That secret would always be dangerously there, like a bomb that might suddenly start ticking again. It and the gambling losses blended and massed together into a dark and heavy weight on me. One thing that was clear in my mind were the numbers. I was down to only $10,000 but owed Carpenter Dave $20,000. I still had my new credit card my grandmother had cosigned for me to use while I was in college. It had a $15,000 credit limit and something else called a cash advance I could use. I thought if need be it would be my lifeline.

Sunday came and I rolled out of bed, not allowing my mind to drift to the dark side of everything that was going wrong. I had wanted to hit the Tiger game and hoped to get myself even. And that game worked out—I had the whole $10,000 on the Tigers—as they stomped their division foe, the Cleveland Indians.

I went to visit Carpenter Dave and place an order for my pharmaceuticals. He seemed reluctant to come through for me on them. I don't know if Tyler's father had got wind of what was going on with me and Carpenter Dave and warned him to cut me off, or if he genuinely cared about my well-being. After assuring him everything was just fine, only a minor setback, he gave me my drugs. I didn't really care what he thought as long as I got what I needed and stayed with my plan. At the high stakes tables, I asked the house to raise the limits to a $5,000 table max.

The roll began with two nice sleeves bumping my chip count of $10,000 up to $40,000. Just as I envisioned, the whole day was working out for me. I took a bathroom break and came back to find two Asian men sitting at my table. I thought a change would probably be good because the table at one and two hands would likely turn. I started at $3,000 for two hands and stayed mostly even for about one hour. Fueled by an endless flow of cocktails I pushed my bets to $5,000 and to two hands. Suddenly, there I was with two splits on each hand with four double downs all totaling 19 against the dealers up card of eight. There was $40,000 on the table; my whole bankroll. I felt certain I was back on top and started thinking of how I was going to enjoy the rest of my night when I cashed this in.

The two chain-smoking Asians were to play their hands after me. The first guy had 20 which prompted a quick hand wave. The next had 16. For some unknown, crazy, reason which is unexplainable or inexcusable, he waved the dealer off as well. The dealer turned over a seven and then pulled a 5 which gave him 20. Heart pounding, my rush turned into bitter despair and rage. I have little recollection of my outburst but I quickly had security guys all over me and they escorted me to my room.

I woke up Monday morning vowing never to play at the same table with anyone ever again. Now, I had one more thing to constantly replay in my mind. It was like a looped tape constantly showing a series of bad events. My bankroll was gone and I still owed Carpenter Dave $10,000. I opened the minibar and started drinking. After emptying what was left of the small bottles, I staggered out into the day and realized I had missed morning classes. I'd have to haul ass to get to Grand Rapids in time for practice.

* * *

GRAND RAPIDS COMMUNITY COLLEGE PRACTICE FIELD

Fucking machine-gun drill, Avery winced as they cut his jersey away and unsnapped his shoulder pads. He had felt it go; that sick shudder vibration like snapping a tree branch over your thigh. Only this was his left collar bone and shoulder joint and much worse than the stingers he had suffered previously.

"How many times?"

Avery looked up at the doctor who had just come into the locker room. "What?" He sat on the training table hunched over, his body wanting to lean to the left, and couldn't straighten his torso.

The doctor gently, for a man who looked like a lumberjack, pulled his sweat soaked t-shirt away to look at the damage. "This is the third time, Avery. We'll get x-rays but I can see already I'm going to have to screw and plate this to get it to hold."

"How long before I can play?"

He shook his head solemnly. "Not this year. You keep reinjuring that shoulder, Avery. It's not going to be the same. Ever." The doctor now looked like he had to tell his best friend that beer no longer existed. "Avery, you keep trying to play before this heals and you're going to end up with a permanent disability. You're risking muscle and nerve damage and that kind of injury means it'll atrophy." He put his hand on Avery's good shoulder. "Look at me, son. I have to tell the coach that your season is over. It's too risky for you to play again this year. But we'll get you on a rehab program to be ready for next year."

* * *

AVERY'S GRANDMOTHER'S HOUSE

AVERY IRONS

Buried in my own little world of worry since the surgery on my shoulder I hadn't checked it in days. My answering machine was lit up with ten messages. I had known before my finger touched the play button who it was. Sure enough, message 1 was, "Hey Avery haven't seen you around lately. You need to get ahold of me." None other than Carpenter Dave's subtle reminder of my outstanding debt. The tone of his voice shifted from one message to the next with escalating irritability. Message 2, "Call me." Message 3, "Ten dimes motherfucker." I erased the rest of them as my grandmother came into the room. I was thankful she never touched anything on the answering machine or paid attention to it.

"Everything okay?" She was worried about my decision to take time off from school while my shoulder healed.

"Sure grandma, just going to take a shower." I went upstairs into my room and sat next to the air conditioner wall unit as I stared out the window. The cool air penetrated my sweaty drenched tee shirt as I contemplated my next move. Right then and there, I realized it. Sure I could use my lifeline/cash advance on my credit card and pay

Carpenter Dave off, but that would mean they got the best of me. There was only one way out of this situation.

I tossed a couple of Darvocet down and stepped into the shower. Being careful of my left shoulder's incision that was healing fast, I rinsed off without any recollection of using shampoo or soap. Totally focused, I went down the stairs, lifting the sports section from the Detroit News on my way out the door. I drove down the street and pulled into the 7-11 and parked next to the payphone. Scanning the betting lines, I reverted back to my old system. Look for the best starting pitcher and bet them hard. Starting with the Detroit Tigers, my man Jack Morris on the hill on the road at Baltimore. There's one lock. Dave Righetti, New York Yankees at home against a struggling Texas Ranger team. Third, Oakland A's Dave Stewart on the road at Toronto. The three best pitchers on the board. Awkwardly, reaching my right hand across my body, I rolled down the window to grab the phone to call Carpenter Dave, a wave of nerves flowed through my fingers as they connected with the numbers that would ring him. My stomach churned as the line rang. A raspy truck driver's voice responded "Hello."

"It's Avery."

"Bout time you called me. You got my money?"

"Yeah, but I want to make a few plays." The line was quiet and I wondered if he'd been cut off or had hung up on me.

"You better have the money. Don't fuck around with me."

"Don't worry I got it."

"Who do you want?"

"Detroit -120 for 10 dimes, New York Yankees -130 for 10 dimes and Oakland -110 for 10 dimes."

Carpenter Dave snorted loudly. "You better have the money to cover these, Avery. I'm not fucking around with this thing. You lose, you better pay up on Monday."

I paused to take in the magnitude of the situation and what I had just put on the line. "You got it, buddy." I hung up and quickly pulled out of the 7-11 parking lot and made my way to I-75. Time to execute the second part of my plan.

* * *

CASINO – FRANK'S PLACE

Avery's 30-minute drive to the casino downtown was occupied with the play by play call of Detroit's own Ernie Harwell. After Chet Lemon had ripped a bases-loaded triple off the left-field wall in the second to take an early 3-0 lead, he felt strong about the game with Jack Morris on the mound. As Avery exited his car at the valet point, he could hear the fountain nearby. He thought to himself, this is the calm before the storm.

At the door, he got a long look at his left arm in the sling and then a nod from the large blond Russian, Boris, to enter the casino floor. He walked directly to the cashier window after swiping his credit card for the full limit of a $15,000 cash advance. His lifeline was now in play. Ready to do battle. The smoke filled establishment was packed as he combed the high stakes Blackjack tables, looking for a seat that would define his existence. He found a table with only one player sitting at 3rd base. A guy he had met once or twice down here but only remembered that he went by the name of Doby. He was a high-strung heavy betting drinker. What he was chasing or running from, he would never know and didn't care.

The table minimum was $1,000 with a maximum of $20,000. Avery started with one eye on the Tigers game and one on his minimum bet of $1,000. For the better part of two hours, his stack fluctuated not able to find any rhythm. Cocktail after cocktail that stack was slowly depleting. The Tigers closed out Baltimore 6-1, which gave him a sense of relief at getting close to even with Carpenter Dave. However, his $15,000 was down to $3,000.

On this table, it was no question that he was the lamb as Doby was hot hitting splits and doubles left and right. His flamboyant behavior drew a lot of attention to their table. Doby relentlessly ordered Crown Royal on the rocks for both of them. With three drinks in him, Avery could feel his polluted body start to sway. As he looked to get a glimpse of his other two games, the pit boss approached Doby.

"Sir we mistakenly paid you on a double-down about half an hour ago. You owe us $10,000 dollars."

"Bullshit."

"We went back and looked at the tape."

"No fucking way, I'm not paying you back for your mistake. That would have changed my whole betting scheme."

Quickly security men surrounded the table with gawkers gathering to watch what was going on behind them.

"You have to pay us back, now, or you'll be escorted out of here. And you won't be able to return."

Doby exclaimed with a drunken slur. "Fine kick me out. It'll give me a reason to quit gambling. You're doing me a favor."

The two security men brought him to his feet and moved him toward the exit.

Avery wasn't sure if they allowed him to cash in his chips before he left. But one thing was sure when Doby left the table shifted in his favor. One golden sleeve after another. He could do no wrong. He pushed his bet to $5,000 a hand and never wavered. Splits turned into double-down 20 and 21's. The dealer could not make a hand even against his poor ones. Bust after bust. He put the dealer into the game to bet along for tips at $500 a hand. The streak went on and on. Avery emptied all of the $1,000 and $5,000 chips from the dealer's chest. After winning all the chips on the reload he told the security guard when he brought more, "That's not enough."

They tried everything to change the flow of the cards by switching dealers multiple times. Nothing worked to derail his hot streak. The pit boss leaned over to Avery and whispered, "You know you could buy a Bentley with those chips."

"Give me another drink I'm going to turn the lights out on this place." Avery did a quick estimate. He thought he had somewhere around $195,000 in front of him. "Now's the time, two hands at $20,000."

Timing is everything and for some unknown reason at that point, his luck went south. His 19, 20 and Blackjacks went to the other side of the table. Double-down 11s got hammered with 2s and 4s. Beginning hands were nothing but 14 and 15s followed by paint. Before he could finish his second drink after declaring himself the new owner of the establishment, he was down to his last two bets. Chips already on the table ahead of the realization of how much of a downturn he had suffered. Nothing in front of him, down to the felt with nothing left but the somber words of the dealer. "Sorry, Sir. Blackjack." It was a double kick in the gut that left Avery breathless. Frank, his casino host, leaned over his shoulder but not to hand him the keys to the front door. It was a room key.

"Tough luck Avery, you really had it rolling. Stay the night with us and sleep it off."

He staggered up to his room with a hollow feeling. The worst he had ever experienced. Usually it didn't hit him until the morning when he opened his eyes and the booze had at least partially metabolized. When his head hit the pillow, it was nothing short of a blackout. He was awakened by a heavy glare raging through the thin draped windows. The same feelings of despair were there but magnified tenfold. He stared at the ceiling and listened to the closing of the heavy guestroom doors as others made their way back to their everyday lives. His life had turned into shit. After an hour or so only one thing came to his mind. He had forgotten about his other two bets on the baseball games. He rushed over to turn the television on to find out his fate. The ticker on the bottom of the screen slowly streamed from left to right. There it was Detroit 6 Baltimore 1, Texas 4 NYY 3, Toronto 2 Oakland 0.

"FUCK!" he looked up and told the ceiling.

Chapter 24

SEPTEMBER 1989
CORNELL UNIVERSITY
SCHOELLKOPF FIELD
ITHACA, NEW YORK

Big Red football wasn't the USC Trojans but Ryan was proud to be playing at his father's alma mater. Despite his father telling him of its rich tradition and history, he still didn't understand why they had an unofficial mascot called 'Touchdown,' the bear. Why couldn't they just be called the Cornell Bears?

Despite being an Ivy League school they were still considered Division I and had produced players that went on to pro careers. His dad still talked about Ed Marinaro, a Cornell running back who had set several records—some collegiate—at Cornell and went on to play six years in the NFL. It could happen. He knew he could play well enough to get a shot at the NFL.

He looked up at the crescent-shaped stands that rose over the field. They would hold over 25,000 spectators and today they were full. A dense field of red-wearing fans. He tugged at the fabric of his carnelian jersey and looked at the helmet in his hands with its white C emblazoned on each side. Kickoff was only minutes away and he was one of only two true freshmen to start the game against Princeton.

Princeton won the coin toss and elected to receive. Ryan trotted onto the field with the coverage team. The butterflies were at home in the pit of his stomach. He always had them. They would settle down after his first hit on an opponent. They always did.

The kick, even into the wind, sailed far. He felt his heart thump with each jarring yard covered until he realized it was caught and kneed down, in the end, zone, for a touchback. He stayed on the field to huddle with the first string defense. He had earned his start as the SAM linebacker on the strong side of the line across from Princeton's tight-end.

He watched them break their huddle and followed their tight-end's alignment. He studied the center, his grip on the ball, in his mind reviewing a flash card summary created from hours of film study of their offense, its tendencies and snap counts. He timed it perfectly, knowing what hole to hit. He met and stood up the tailback coming through and drove him backward for no gain. He hardly felt or heard his teammates congratulating him in the huddle for the next play.

It was second down and 10. He saw the tight-end shift and move too wide to the outside. He cut inside him to slam the tailback down for a 1-yard loss.

After months of not playing it was everything he loved about the game and more. The smell and feel of the turf, the color of the sky overhead, everything was sharper and clearer when he was on a football field. He heard every one of the 25,512 people in the stands as they stomped and cheered.

It was third and 11. The ball was snapped and he surged toward the quarterback who was dropping back to pass. Their tight-end had him blocked high as he drove him into the backfield. Somehow he had bit his inner cheek or busted a lip and now tasted coppery blood in his mouth. He wanted to replace it with the taste of his first sack as a college football player. He bucked and shoved and was about to shed the tight-end's block when he felt a blinding, ripping, pain in his left knee. He felt it give away and buckle at an angle it shouldn't bend at. Princeton's 265-pound right guard had chopped him low. He saw the ball leave the quarterback's hand as he went to the turf writhing in agony. He gripped his left knee and tried to hold it together but it felt as if it had come apart inside. The tears came as he spat out his bloody mouthpiece. He felt his stomach heave and bile mixed with blood on the turf. Christ, oh Christ it hurt.

* * *

They had carried him into the locker room and one of the trainers and the team doctor had checked his knee. The doctor shook his head and all he would say as they packed his knee in ice and issued a set of crutches was, "We'll get you to an orthopedic specialist to check the extent of the damage."

The next day later he had undergone a series of x-rays and scans. Two days after that he sat at the Orthopedic Surgical Center listening to something he couldn't believe he was hearing. It was going to take major surgery to put it back together. Everything in his knee had been destroyed and it would take at least a year to rehab.

The wet sidewalk was slick and he almost busted his ass as he left the medical building. That would really top things off, he thought. If I fall and break something, then maybe I can get a two for one in surgery. Then the realization set in. The doctor had refused to say anything about playing next year. He had told Ryan, "Let's get that knee opened up and see what we've got to fix first."

* * *

OCTOBER 1989

CORNELL UNIVERSITY DORMITORY

"Kramer, it's for you." The upperclassman stuck his head into his dorm room.

With a groan, Ryan got up from his desk using his crutches to lever himself erect. Those pain meds suck, he thought as he took a deep breath. He carefully swung around and worked his left leg from under the desk clearing the chair legs with a sigh. Damn, it hurt.

"Thanks." He took the phone from the impatient student in the hall. "This is Ryan."

"So how bad did you fuck up your knee?" It was Tyler. He had not seen or talked to him since that night back home at the spa and gym he'd been managing before he moved into the city.

"After it happened I tried to get up on it and it folded like an empty sock. I looked down and my foot was backward and the leg was bent at the knee to the right at an angle." He heard Tyler take a deep breath. "ACL, MCL, completely torn with other cartilage and the joint damaged. The doctors say it's catastrophic."

"When I heard about what had happened I had to call you. Your mom wasn't too pleased to see me but she gave me your number."

The leg throbbed, even more, when standing. "Shit, Tyler. Everyone's heard you're dealing drugs and beating the fuck out of people that owe money to their supplier."

He didn't reply to that and asked him, "Do you think you'll rehab in time to play next year?"

"I'll be lucky if I can end up feeling and moving my toes." He paused and felt the bile rise in his throat. He hadn't said these words to anyone yet. "There's nerve damage and I'll never be able to play football again."

Tyler knew the pain his friend felt just saying that was worse than what he felt hearing it. "I'm sorry Ryan."

Ryan shifted his crutches under his arm and leaned his head against the wall, still holding the phone to his ear. Tyler sounded like he was concerned and he sounded as if he cared. Right then he sounded like the 14-year-old Tyler that would become his best friend. The friend who shared a dream of playing in the NFL, too. And in his tone was something else. He sounded like he regretted the way things had worked out—for him—for all of them.

"Tyler, stop what you're doing and go home. Your dad can help you work things out. Hell, find a college over here you can get into and maybe we can split an apartment."

"You don't understand Ryan. It's not that simple. I can't just do that; not with the people I work for. Not now."

"Get out of Detroit, Tyler. You can change things. But--"

He cut him off. "It's the money, Ryan, and the rush. I have to have it... just like when we played." Ryan could hear this voice change into the Tyler he'd last talked to behind the spa and gym in Shelby. "Don't tell me what to do... you got problems of your own."

The line went dead. Ryan stared at it for a moment and then hung up the phone. He slowly pivoted to return to his room. He wondered that, even though not in touch like maybe they should be, an old friend still had reached out to see how he was doing. That's not the feeling he got on campus and with his new teammates. Once he was hurt, his value to them all dropped and he was just another student. Thankfully, since he was injured while playing, his scholarship held and would continue but school administration had already advised him that he had to meet their academic requirements for non-athlete students on scholarship and now that he couldn't play none of the professors would cut him any slack.

Chapter 25

**NOVEMBER 1989
THE UNIVERSITY OF SOUTHERN CALIFORNIA
CAMPUS
LOS ANGELES, CALIFORNIA**

JACOB WINSLOW

When I had arrived at USC everything felt right. I kept telling myself it was the first chapter of my new life. It felt like a new beginning for me.

I had passed all my physical examinations and initial fitness testing: my mile time, 5 minutes 20 seconds—40-yard dash, 4.7 seconds and bench press, 225 pounds 13 reps. My competition was the current starter, Mike Churchill a senior, Javon Speeks, a sophomore with lightning speed and two other incoming freshmen, Rick O'Mara from Kansas and Jared Sessions from northern California.

Within a few weeks of practice my arm strength and accuracy were better than the others and I was getting noticed. But it still looked like three of us would compete for the backup quarterback spot behind Churchill, who was more experienced in the offense. I was climbing the depth chart fast and got the sense that Mike Churchill was looking over his shoulder keeping an eye on me. The tough two a day practice schedule and endless film study left little time to think about the past. I missed my friends, but my new life was taking shape in a way that I enjoyed even more than I had imagined back in Michigan. In practices, I quickly went from the scout team to running the second offense before our home opener with Notre Dame. Getting redshirted my first year was not going to happen.

Our head coach called me in his office the Thursday before our first Saturday night game with the Irish. Coach Riley was behind his desk. "Sit down Jacob. You're quite a talent. Now, this is Mike's team but I want you to be ready to go at any time." He put his hands flat on the desk and looked me in the eye. "I need someone behind Mike that I can count on when I need him."

I thought about that through the beginning of the season. Even when Mike threw three interceptions in a terrible loss to Notre Dame in our first game, I remained on the sidelines. The next five games were tight but we managed to pull off victories. Other than in warm-ups I wasn't on the field. Then came the Stanford game on Halloween night.

We were up 28 to 7 with nine minutes and 46 seconds left in the fourth quarter when my number was called and I made my college debut. I figured I would be handing the ball off until time expired. I was wrong. Coach Riley didn't close the playbook. Instead, he opened up our vertical game. I went 13 of 14 on two drives of 80 yards and threw two touchdowns. I felt an incredible rush and feeling of empowerment over my first action at the collegiate level. I knew it was mop up duty, but I was able to display pinpoint accuracy with unmatched velocity. Mike Churchill got the win as the starter, but I showed what I could do if given some playing time.

I didn't hear it during the game, but saw the sports news later when one of the announcers turned to the other and said about me: "This young man, right in front of us, is the future of Trojan football for the next four years." I called home that night and found that my father had taped the game and was going to send me a copy. He was probably the only one up or sober that late on a Saturday night after watching my game on television.

Later in the week leading up to the UCLA game I did get a call of congratulation from Ryan. I had not talked to him since hearing how he had blown his knee out in his first game. He told me he was concerned about Avery and Tyler. Their self-destructive habits had escalated and they were clearly unraveling. He didn't know where things would end up for them, but it didn't look good. Maybe it was karma from what had happened at Torch Lake starting to rip into our new lives. Or maybe for me, it was having the opposite effect since I had wanted to do the right thing and go to the police immediately. The conversation with Ryan made me worry all over again about waiting and wondering if we would end up in jail or suffer some consequences of what had happened that night. It was always in the back of my mind.

But for now, it looked like we had gotten away with it and the devil hadn't come to call on me to collect that debt. In my life things were all on the up and up and going my way. But I knew as a friend I should reach out to Avery and Tyler and check on them. I knew Tyler would never talk and hopefully Avery was not breaking down to the point where he needed to confess and turn us in to save his soul. I never thought I would have to worry about one of us breaking our agreement to keep quiet. Now I was.

Chapter 26

LATE FALL 1990
TYLER'S OFFICE (FORMERLY CARLOS
HERMOSA'S)
DETROIT

Things had grown so well, so fast, that Tyler was solidly entrenched as one of the top dealers in Metropolitan Detroit. So much so that Carlos had let him run operations there when he relocated to Mexico to play a larger role on the supply side.

Maybe it was reading the sports page about USC and their hot sophomore starting quarterback, Jacob Winslow, that decided it for him. Jacob was tearing up the conference and USC was ranked number one. He was going to move on and in a couple of years would hit the NFL draft; the big-time they had all dreamed of as football players. Or maybe it was he remembered the last time he had talked to Ryan. Someone he always thought of like his brother and he had asked him what in hell he was doing dealing drugs. None of them understood the situation. Of all of them, he was the one that hadn't had an opportunity offered to him. He had gone out and created one. Just like his father had done when he needed to. And this—the deal with Carlos—was his opportunity. Another year had cemented things with him. Fuck it, he thought, I'm all in.

* * *

JUNE 1991
INTERNATIONAL AIRPORT

MONTERREY, MEXICO
TYLER JENNELO

Over the past several months the profits had climbed even further without any extra exposure or risk. Carlos had asked me again to come to Mexico and meet with him. "You've earned more opportunity, my young friend. I have some interesting developments that I think you'll want to be a part of."

I knew what kind of man Carlos was. I'd had thoughts over the last year about separating from him, but the money was too damn good. Maybe this new development would be an even bigger payday—the kind that could help me take my money and run. I called Carlos back and told him I would fly down.

I deplaned in Monterrey, Mexico where I was to make a connecting flight. This was my third trip to Mexico and first time through this airport. I looked around for a place to get a beer in Terminal B while I waited for my Aeromexico flight. I spotted The Blue Sky Bar, went in and found a seat at a window looking out on the tarmac. I positioned my carry-on bag against the wall under the table and slipped the strap of my shoulder bag over the chair back next to me. As I sat a young woman—though she was probably three or four years older than me—came to the table.

"May I get you a drink, señor?" She smiled with perfect teeth that gleamed even whiter against a dark-complexioned, lovely, face framed by jet black hair.

I had studied my Mexican beers. "Negra Modelo por favor, on draft if you have it."

She smiled at me and nodded. "Si, I'll be back shortly with it." Soon she was and brought a menu with it. She set both on the table in front of me. "Would you like to order something to eat?"

I rotated the handle of the frosty mug toward me and lifted. The first sip was excellent; ice cold. I shook my head. "Not yet, I'll be here a while so maybe later. Okay?"

Her smile widened for me. "My name is Gabriella if you need anything... I'll check back with you in a few minutes."

I watched her walk away and the swaying of her long black hair, done in a French braid, made me think of my last trip to Mexico. It had been at the request of Carlos, basically another one of his tests that I had successfully passed. It surely had led to the extra money I'd made since and to the opportunity that Carlos had mentioned to me but wouldn't reveal until we met face-to-face on this trip.

I drank off the top third of the mug and settled back in my chair. I glanced around the bar, eyes passing over its handful of customers, and saw Gabriella flash that smile at me again from behind the bar. As she turned away the swing of her long twist of hair reminded me of the woman Carlos had sent me, on my first trip to Mexico, to escort back to the United States as her American boyfriend:

Carlos, during our routine Sunday night conversation to go over weekly numbers, had asked me at the end of the call. "How would you like to spend a week in Puerto Vallarta where you will be joined by a lovely, older, woman?"

I, by then, knew there was always something that Carlos wanted when he offered you anything. "What is it that you need me to do?" I had replied.

"I'll send you a round-trip ticket to leave next Wednesday. I have reservations at the Lindo Mar, an older resort that's away from the newer developments around the city. There you will be joined by Juanita Dellamer."

"Who is she?" I had asked him.

"It has to do with limited runs of some high-grade merchandise—our highest value per pound product—to be sold in an exclusive market. I don't want to use our normal delivery channels."

I realized Carlos wasn't going to tell me who she was. "What am I supposed to do with her?"

Carlos had laughed in that way that told me he was deadly serious. "Enjoy her company for a week and then return to Detroit with her. I'll be here then to meet you both." I didn't answer immediately. I was thinking things through since I didn't trust him. "Well?" He had prodded me. "Do you want to do this little thing for me?"

I knew that this wasn't some small task. It was Carlos testing me as much is it was anything else. "Okay, I'll do it."

"Excellent, my young friend. One thing more. If anyone appears who wishes to stop this little experiment, do not let them. Understand?"

I had already been bloodied on some of Carlos's collections and wasn't surprised. "I understand; no problem." I was about to hang up when he added a comment I wouldn't understand until a week later.

"And my friend you can fuck Juanita, but don't touch her tits." With another coarse laugh, he hung up the phone. As odd and off-hand as the comment seemed, I knew that he meant it.

A couple of days later I received the package of an airplane ticket and reservation information from Carlos. Then the following Wednesday I had flown from Detroit to Houston, Texas and from there to Puerto Vallarta on the Mexican Pacific coast. From the airport, it was a 30-minute taxi ride to the shore area south of the city. When I checked in I had found that Juanita was already there. I went to our room and knocked. The woman that answered was probably in her late 30s and was dressed expensively. Her face was average, kind of plain actually. But she had a knockout body.

The room contained a full bar and a complete line of recreational pharmaceuticals. We partied and fucked for three days and not once did I see her naked. She was nervous at first—sensitive if my hands strayed toward her chest—but I stayed clear just as Carlos had warned me. It wasn't until the fourth night that I found out why when I caught her injecting what I learned was a surgical anesthetic underneath each breast where two incisions were half-healed. She looked at me and, at first, I didn't think that she would explain since I hadn't questioned anything. She gingerly put two pieces of foam support under each breast and then carefully wrapped her chest to hold them in place.

"In another two or three days I can easily travel." She went from the bathroom to the bar and poured shots of tequila, Fortaleza extra-Anejo.

"What's going on?" I gestured at her breasts knowing that this was more than just escorting some woman who had a tit job from Mexico to the United States.

She downed the tequila and turned to me. "I'm carrying two pounds of high-grade cocaine, in bags, inside my breasts. In America, they'll take them out and replace with silicone."

"Are you part of Carlos's organization?"

She shook her head and a look of something more than pain flashed in her eyes. "Carlos asked me to do this... And you know how it is when he asks something of you. Don't you?"

I nodded and took the other shot of tequila that she handed to me and downed it. "What would happen if you didn't..." I looked from her breasts to her face. "Didn't do this for him?"

She walked over and drew back the drapes for the balcony. The sun was setting. "He thinks he can use Hispanic-American women, dress them well and send them to Mexico for cosmetic surgery and the implants they return with contain his most valuable product. He thinks Customs and DEA will never squeeze or check a rich woman's new tits." A breeze from the bay caught and lifted her hair as she turned back to face me. "If I don't do this for him, Carlos will kill my family."

The next three days I didn't touch her. It seemed wrong to continue to, as we waited for the return flights back to the United States. The days had seemed long. Finally, we made it back passing smoothly through customs as the affluent Hispanic woman with her American boy-toy. In Detroit, at the airport one of Carlos's men met us and took her with him. As she walked away, she looked over her shoulder at me as her French braid swayed back and forth. I picked up my car from the parking garage. When I got to Carlos's office, she wasn't there and I would never see her again.

"Would you like another beer, señor?" Gabriella was beside the table and startled me.

I shook myself out of that memory. "Yes please." She headed to the bar and I looked around again. There were still only a few other customers. I recognized the song that was playing, *Creep* by Radiohead. I don't know why but I suddenly thought of Ryan. Still in college but he would never play football again. Never be the Ryan I played side by side with for years. I remembered how once all we wanted to do was play football. On the playing field, we were someone… we were something special. I was part of something I was proud of and now, I wasn't anymore. What the fuck had I turned into? "I wish I was special… But, I'm a creep… I'm a weirdo."

"What was that señor?" Gabriella had a puzzled, questioning, look on her face and a mug of beer in her hand.

I realized she had overheard me as I quietly sang that line from the song. I looked up at her and took the beer she offered. "Nothing. It was nothing." I drank deep and then looked at my watch. An hour and 45 minutes to go until it was time to board my next flight.

* * *

CULIACAN, SINALOA
MEXICO

Tyler looked out the window of the limo Carlos had sent to pick him up at the airport. He watched the raggedy kids, mostly boys but a few girls, playing soccer with the scuffed beat-up ball. He looked at their faces. They all smiled and laughed and cheered. Behind them, he saw adults lean in their doorways or back against a wall watching them play. Clouds of dirt and dust billowed and covered them but no one

157

seemed to mind. He remembered what it was like playing football and feeling that same way. Nothing else mattered but being on the field with his teammates. Nothing. And that had gotten all fucked up. He shook his head and asked the driver. "How much longer?"

"Ten... maybe 15 minutes, señor."

Tyler reclined into the deep cushions. The cold bottle of Negra Modelo in his hand sweated with condensation. He rubbed it against his forehead and felt its coolness, then took a big drink. Ice cold. He closed his eyes. Twenty minutes later he held another fresh, cold, beer and was sitting in front of Carlos's huge mahogany desk.

Chapter 27

JUNE 1991
CARLOS HERMOSA'S OFFICE
THE SINALOA CARTEL

"So things are going well in Detroit?" Carlos Hermosa now wore a $2,000 suit.

Tyler's suit wasn't quite that expensive. "Yes. Distribution has broadened and collections are in good shape to keep the cash flowing." He ran his fingers along the silk of his tie. "You said you were looking at expanding and wanted to know if I'd be interested. Why did I have to come all the way down here to see if I am and to talk to you about it?"

Carlos took out a photo album and slid it across the desk toward Tyler. "It's a multi-billion dollar a year industry and I want a piece of it." He reached across and flipped the cover open and on the first page were pictures of four young girls with information and numbers underneath. The binder must've contained 40 or 50 pages. "This is the inventory I can access. It's like buying gold for a dollar and selling it for $100."

Tyler didn't say anything as he looked up from the album at Carlos.

"Didn't you tell me you wanted to be a rich man? You wanted to have more money and more power than your old man." He saw the look on Tyler's face. "Oh yeah, I told you I know how he made his money and what he does. In a lot of ways, he trafficks, too." He spun the album around and flipped through the pages, then closed and pushed it to one side. "I've got more buyers than inventory but I need a hard man, someone who doesn't take shit from anyone, who can handle the delivery and the buyers if they stir anything up." He looked at Tyler. "You're not talking so I'm gonna assume that means you're thinking. I'll tell you what. I got you a suite at the best place in town. Molina here will drive you over there shortly." He gestured at the stocky man standing in the shadows of the corner. "I'll send you a little treat and then I want you to think about what I'm offering and we'll talk some more tomorrow."

* * *

HOTEL LUCERNA CULIACAN

Tyler picked up a slice of lime and dropped it into the frosted glass of another Negra Modelo they'd stocked his room with. He struggled with what Carlos had told him in his office only an hour before. He knew that Carlos didn't offer things to people only to be refused. You either took him up on the offer or you disappeared. He didn't hold any illusions that because he had done so well for Carlos and made Carlos so much more money than Gavin had that it would mean much to him.

He didn't have enough formal knowledge to figure out the distinction between the two but he suspected that Carlos was either a sociopath or full-blown psychopath. He had heard about the girls that Carlos ran in Detroit, the ages of some of them and how many that had simply disappeared when they were worn out. All of them long before their time. That wasn't his thing and he hadn't wanted to know any details. All he wanted was to do what he was doing and make his money and keep sticking it in the bank and then someday have enough to get out and go legitimate. Maybe buy into or start some sports related business.

What Carlos had in those folders, what he was planning to do and that he wanted him involved, changed everything. He couldn't ignore any longer the other things that went on in Carlos operations. He thought again about sitting in that bar at the Monterrey airport… that song and what he had reflected on. He was disgusted with himself in a way that he hadn't been ever in his life.

There was a knock on the door and a soft voice that he couldn't hear clearly through it. He walked over to look through the peephole and all he could see was the top of the head of what looked to be a dark-haired young lady. He opened the door a six-inch crack. "Whatever it is I don't want any." He could see her face. It had too much make up for his tastes. The girl stood there in her short skirt and tight t-shirt and shifted from foot to foot.

"Carlos says that I am for you tonight." She didn't sound like she looked forward to it. She said it flatly with just a hint of a quiver in her voice.

Tyler opened the door but didn't step away so she could enter. He looked at her. She was pretty, with long legs accented by the short skirt and a tight t-shirt showing a well-rounded, full, figure. "What's your name?"

"It's whatever you'd like it to be, señor."

Again the shake in her voice and it sounded like what she had said came from a script or what someone had told her to say when she was asked her name. She had started moving slightly, very small steps from side to side, and he wondered why. Then he looked closer in her eyes and he knew. He'd seen it in guys on the street who had run out of cash or credit and couldn't get what they needed. They danced and jittered in place; their nerves jumping. He saw her look to her left then to her right and then back to her left toward the end of the hall. "Please, if I don't come in with you they'll find someone else for me. And if too many don't like me—don't take me—then..." She looked scared and her voice had a strained pitch to it.

"Okay. Come in, but were not doing anything. You understand?" Tyler backed away from the door and the girl stepped inside.

He pointed at one of the chairs next to the table. "Go ahead and sit down."

She looked from him to the bed and then back at him. "You do not want me there?" She pointed at the bed.

"I told you I don't want you at all but I'll let you in because you seem scared." Tyler sat in the chair opposite the one he had invited her to sit in and picked up his glass of beer. "How old are you?"

She stood there looking at him. "How old do you want me to be, señor?"

Again, that came out as a script they had taught her to follow. In the brighter light in his room, he could now see how young she really was. He looked at her arms and saw where she'd used makeup to cover the needle tracks.

"I don't want you to be anything. I told you I don't want you for sex. So why don't you sit down and try to relax? I'm not going to touch you."

She sat down, her legs tightly together. On the outside of them above her knees, he saw the bruising that had also been covered by makeup.

"What's your real name? Not a pretend name. Your real name."

She had a questioning look on her face when he still made no move toward her. "My name is Carla."

"Carla, is there someone watching you outside my room?"

"There was." She nodded. "But they leave if I go into a room and then watch downstairs for when I come out."

Tyler looked at her and for some reason thought of Shelley. There was something in Carla's eyes that told him she was as young as Shelley had been when they met and started dating their sophomore year of high school. Carla was too young for what she was doing and no girl deserved what had happened—what was happening—to her. He looked again at her arms and the mottled, yellowing, bruises on her legs. He closed his eyes, thinking of the last time he had seen Shelley's face, bruised and battered, through Amanda's apartment door and leaned back. He heard a scraping sound and opened them.

Carla had risen and with her head down was now standing beside the bed. "What are you doing?" he asked her.

She was shaking so slightly that he could only tell by the swaying of the long strands of hair that covered her face. "Sometimes, at first, they don't want to but then—especially the older men—they change their mind. I see them thinking and they close their eyes. And then they take me."

Tyler felt the anger beginning to boil inside him. It always tended to be there and not too far beneath the surface but this time, it was different. It was there but it wasn't the self-indulgent hurt little boy lashing out that usually manifested in himself. This almost felt like what he'd read about and even made fun of: righteous indignation. He couldn't understand how anyone could hurt a young girl like this. And do the things that had been done to her. He saw her watching him from her lowered eyes and slowed his breathing. He didn't need to frighten her any more than she already was. "I'm not going to hurt you. I'm not going to touch you. Please," he pointed at the chair again. "Sit down."

She did and watched him as if he was something new. Something she'd either not seen before or not seen in a very long time. "What do you want me to do then?"

Tyler sighed because he didn't know what to do with her. "I just want you to sit there and relax and not worry about me. Let me ask you this. I don't want to know how you ended up doing what you're doing but I know you're being made to. Right?"

She nodded. "Carlos... Well, not him but by his men. And Carlos always has first night with each of us." She lowered her head again. She had her arms crossed and he watched as she rubbed the line of needle marks on their inside where the elbow bends.

"Do you have any family?"

She shook her head.

"Not just here. Anywhere?"

"I have two aunts and cousins in El Paso."

"If I give you money can you get away from here and make your way to El Paso?"

"The coyotes, the cross-border smugglers, I know some of them. I could find one that would take me but I think it costs $8,000. I'm not sure."

Tyler got up out of the chair noticing that she flinched slightly as he walked over to his bag. He reached inside a zippered compartment and took out a banded stack of $100 bills. The strapping label was blank but written across it in red was $10,000. "Are you able to get away from whoever it is that's watching you?"

She nodded. "He is fat and sometimes falls asleep. I can sneak past him."

"Can you get by without a fix long enough to get to El Paso?" Tyler held the stack of strapped bills in his hand watching her eyes closely.

She met his look. Her lips, that had been compressed into a tight line as she studied him, eased. She nodded her head. "Yes. I can, señor."

Tyler looked at her and put the $10,000 on the table between them. He pointed at it. "We're just going to sit here for a while and then I want you to take that..." He tapped the stack of $100 bills. "And get as far from here as you can. And if you are able to get to your family in El Paso." He tucked a business card under the strap. "Call and let me know. My name and phone number is on this card."

She nodded and finally relaxed a bit sitting back in her chair. Taking the wig from her head, she hung it over the back of the chair beside her. Tyler studied her close-cropped dark hair but didn't say anything. She noticed his look. "They shave our heads so they can dress us to fit the customer." She flipped the long, dark, locks of the hairpiece. "Sometimes, old men..." she shivered "want pigtails or maybe they want a blonde." She closed her eyes and he barely heard her. "We get made into what they want us to be... what'll sell..."

Tyler leaned against the wall and looked at her hairpiece hanging from the chair in front of him. He thought of something he hadn't heard in a while but had loved at the time. There was a line in that song, *Jane Says* that always stuck in his mind. He whisper-sang it, "Have you seen my wig around? I feel naked without it..."

"What?" Her voice sounded muffled. He looked up at her and saw that she had been crying but silently, the way you do when you don't want anyone to hear or you know that no one cares anyway.

"Nothing, just a song." He had never seen eyes that had the look of someone so lost. Someone so alone. More of the song came to him, "Starts to cry. She takes a swing but she can't hit. She don't mean no harm. She just don't know what else to do about it." This time, he heard her sobs but he didn't look up. His mind shifted to the song he'd heard in the airport bar in Monterrey. "Couldn't look you in the eye, you're just like an angel, your skin makes me cry, you float like a feather, in a beautiful world." He shook his head and muttered. "What the hell am I doing here?"

* * *

It was a little after 4:00 AM and the girl had been gone for about an hour. He hoped that she made it. He opened the top on another bottle of beer and didn't bother with the glass. He bent over the table where there were four long, pure white, lines. A couple of seconds later he had run them and dabbed a finger at his nose. After setting his bottle down, he went to the bathroom and splashed his face with cold water. In three hours or so he would be having breakfast with Carlos and he wasn't sure whether it might be the last for one of them.

* * *

THAT MORNING, AFTER SUNRISE
CARLOS HERMOSA'S OFFICE

The sun was already bright and strong rising over the horizon and just over the balustrade of the terrace where they sat facing it. Tyler had wondered whether Carlos's fat slave watcher would report her missing. But the look on Carlos' face and the easiness of the men around him indicated that no one had sounded an alarm about a missing girl. Good, Tyler thought.

"I see you are smiling this morning, my young friend." Carlos set his empty coffee cup down and beckoned to the young girl to bring more.

Tyler shrugged looking at Carlos but didn't say anything.

"Have you given any more thought to my proposal—to your involvement—for expanding your fortunes in the business venture I mentioned to you?"

It wasn't on the table like it had been last time they discussed Tyler working for him. But he could see it as if there was really a pistol spinning on the table with Carlos waiting to see where the muzzle pointed. "I have."

Carlos looked at him and widened his eyes expecting more of a response. When he didn't get it, his gaze on Tyler hardened. The parallel lines on his forehead deepened. "And?"

"Why does it have to be young girls?"

"What do you mean?" Carlos looked puzzled.

Before leaving Detroit, Tyler had bought an authentic model 1911a, slab-sided,_.45 caliber automatic. For the very reason that it was flat and not as bulky as the modern handguns, he had learned to handle since he started working for Carlos. But it still stabbed him and poked him in the back where it was tucked in his pants underneath his loose shirt. Thankfully, he had established himself so well with Carlos that his men no longer searched him when they were together. Tyler leaned forward in his chair and shifted. "I mean there's so much money to be made with the drugs. Why girls... Why young, underage, girls?"

Carlos put his forearms up on the table and steepled his fingers. "Because they make much more money than the old ones." He smiled.

"I can't do it, Carlos. I'll distribute the drugs for you. I'll help you sell more. And I'll help you collect from the guys on the street that owe you money. I'll keep that cash flowing for you. But I don't want any part of selling young girls."

Tyler saw a short, heavyweight, man approaching their table. He had already sweated completely through his shirt though it was so early in the day. One of Carlos' men, about 15 feet away stopped him and looked over at Carlos. Carlos nodded and they let the man approach. The man gave Tyler a look and then went to Carlos and bending down said something that Tyler couldn't hear. Carlos nodded and waved the man away. With a final glare at Tyler, the man waddled away as fast as his fat legs would take him.

Carlos looked at Tyler and his hands slowly spun a butter knife on the table. "It seems one of my assets—one of my newest investments—disappeared in the early hours of the morning. She was so sweet; I still have the taste of her on my lips from her first night with us."

Tyler felt the muscles in his abdomen bunch and tense. He lowered his right hand to his lap and then slowly, a half-inch at a time, moved it to his hip just underneath the tail of his shirt.

Carlos watched him with narrowed eyes. "Is some girl that you don't even know worth jeopardizing everything that I've given you? The opportunity. The money. Yes, all the money that you've made working for me."

Tyler felt an adrenaline rush he hadn't felt since the Catholic Central playoff game. It burned a clear path in his thinking and he realized all the times when he'd lost his temper it was for the wrong reasons and always had the worst results. And most times it wasn't just him that got hurt or that suffered the consequences. The single, worst, example of his inability to control his temper had scarred and damaged his friends for the rest of their lives. He was really the guilty one for what happened at Torch Lake and had denied it. But his friends had never accused him... never abandoned him or turned him over to the police—shifting the blame solely onto him—to try and wash their own conscience clean. The power of finally doing something right surged through him.

He shook his head. "Carlos, helping that young girl—if she can get away and maybe have a normal life if that's possible—is worth it." His right hand gripped the pistol. What he was about to do was crazy and against every self-interested bone in his body. But he was still going to do it. He brought the gun from behind him, still low, and began to raise it.

Carlos fired his own from the underside of the table. It grazed Tyler just above his left eye blowing a chunk of his brow away. The three men on the terrace pulled their weapons and Tyler didn't have a chance. They pumped more rounds into him and as he went down, he thought about his father, Ryan, Avery, and Jacob. He thought of a long green field, on a sunny bright blue sky, championship game day, and a ball sailing through the air that he grabbed and ran with... no one could stop him. He got past the last man and ran... and ran. He scored the winning touchdown.

Chapter 28

LATE JUNE 1991
THE NINES RESTAURANT
ITHACA, NEW YORK

Ryan had just picked up the order for table 5 when Samantha leaned out of the office door. "Hey, Ryan. I just took a message for you from some girl named Amanda. She left a number and wants you to give her a call as soon as you can. She said it's important." Samantha seemed disappointed or hurt about the message but then she'd been chasing after him since he came to work there. But he was just too damn busy working two jobs after coming off the physical therapy and the rehab on his left knee. There just wasn't time and he had bills to pay.

"Thanks. Can you clip that to my timecard and I'll call her when I take my break."

Twenty minutes later he dialed her from the payphone by the back door covering one ear because of the clanging and clashing metal pans coming from Tommy in the dish pit. Someone picked up the phone. "Amanda?"

"Yes?" There was a pause and then recognition. "Ryan!"

"Hey, yeah it's me. What's up? I got your message. Are you okay?"

He heard her take a deep breath. "Tyler's dead. It happened in Mexico earlier this month and his dad pulled some strings and got his body home while they investigate what happened. They're having the service July 1st. I thought you should know."

Ryan was stunned. He always thought that someday somehow something would happen to Tyler. He was just too wild. But still he was surprised. He had not talked to him for a long time. The last time had been when Tyler had reached out to him about his knee injury and they had argued over the fact that Tyler was heavily into dealing drugs. They hadn't talked since. "I don't have his father's phone number anymore; can you get it for me?"

"Sure." He heard shuffling. She must be looking in the phone book. "Okay, here it is, bar first then his house."

He jotted down the numbers on the back of the message slip. "I'm gonna give him a call right now and get details but I'll be at the service. Are you going to it?"

He heard her deep breath again and she let it out slowly. "Yes. I'll be there."

It seemed that there was something that she wanted to say but it wouldn't come out. He knew that there was a lot that he wanted to tell her but couldn't. "Okay. Then I'll see you when I get in town. Okay?"

"Sure; I'll see you then." There was a pause and he thought they'd been disconnected. "Bye, Ryan."

"Goodbye... Thanks for letting me know, Amanda." He thought he had said the last part to someone that wasn't on the line anymore. He knew he should have called or at least written her when he first got to Cornell. Then he got hurt and didn't want it to seem like he was contacting her just to be pitied. He hadn't known what to tell her then and still didn't now.

The phone in his hand was giving that off-the-hook buzzing sound. He pressed the hook to clear it then dialed The Wolverine's number first. "Hi. Is Mr. Jennelo in? I understand, but I think he might take my call. Please tell him it's Ryan Kramer." He heard the clatter of someone sitting the phone down, probably on the bar since he heard the clink of nearby glasses and mugs on its surface. Someone picked it up. "I got it, Lou." Ryan heard the noise on the line stop as the bartender hung up his phone when Rick Jennelo took the call in his office.

"Ryan?"

"Yes, Mr. Jennelo. I am so sorry to hear about Tyler. I apologize that I can't talk long because I'm on my work break but I wanted to get some details from you on when the service is going to be held and where. Yes, sir." Ryan scribbled on the slip of paper in his hand. "I'll be there I'll get into town the day before and I'd like to come by and see you then if you don't mind. And sir, I've lost touch with him but do you happen to know where Avery is? I know he dropped out of Grand Rapids when his grandmother passed away but I wasn't able to get to the funeral. Yes, sir, it was about the time I was dealing with my knee injury. I tried to reach him then but wasn't able and his phone's been disconnected. Yes, sir another phone number or address if you have it I'll leave early from here to give me time in Detroit to find Avery and let him know. Here's my phone number at my apartment. I work a lot so if I'm not there if you would just leave it on my answering machine. Thank you, sir. And I'm very sorry about Tyler."

Chapter 29

LATE JUNE 1991
THE WOLVERINE BAR
DETROIT – EAST SIDE

Rick Jennelo was on the speaker phone in his office as he paced. "Frank, I know it's not something you're involved in directly but I need to talk to someone in the Bratva about a cartel cutting in on their trade.

"Rick, you don't want to deal with them. One touch and you will never get clean. You are never not obligated to them in some way once you start. The Solntveskya Bratva, the Brotherhood, connections are forever—until you die or they kill you—and they are everywhere. You can never get away from them."

"That doesn't matter to me. My son, Tyler, got entangled with the cartel and their former head here in Detroit killed him in Mexico. I can't let that stand. That motherfucker's got to come back here to take care of business and I need their help to find out when and where." The line was quiet but he could hear Frank breathing. "I know the Brotherhood already has a reason to be concerned about the Sinaloa Cartel. They've been steadily cutting into their different lines of business. I'm sure they're not happy about that and plan to do something. I want to be just enough a part of that to avenge Tyler."

Frank sighed. "Like I just told you, once you're connected you stay connected. You can't just use them and think that it's over and done with when you get your payback for Tyler."

"I understand." And he did. Once into it, his hands just wouldn't be dirty they'd be bloody. But he'd never live with himself if he didn't get vengeance. He had let Tyler down in many ways when he was alive and he sure as hell wasn't going to do it now that he was dead. He owed his son that. "A week after authorities notified me that Mexican police had found Tyler's body I got a call from a young girl who tracked me down worried because she had not been able to reach Tyler to thank him. She told me what she meant by that." He paused to breathe deeply. "I'm going to kill the cocksucker that killed my son and I think the Bratva may want to help and send a message to the cartel. Frank, it's about respect. I think they'll understand the need for that."

* * *

THE WOLVERINE BAR

The five men weren't typical organized crime street thugs. They all had the build and movement of trained fighters—former Soviet special forces. Rick Jennelo was surprised to see Boris leading them.

He grinned at Rick. "You maybe thought I was just a doorman, Mr. Jennelo?"

Rick shook his head. "I knew you weren't a man to be messed with Boris." He shook his hand. "I take it you're the eyes the Bratva keeps on Frank?"

"And the hands if need be." Boris nodded.

Rick dry-wiped his face with his hands. "So this Carlos is going to be at that warehouse outside of Roseville at midnight?"

"Yes, and we will call on him to welcome him back to Detroit." Boris's mirthless grin showed two rows of perfect, ivory colored, teeth. "Mr. Jennelo..." he paused and Rick looked up at him. "I liked your son. He was wild, yes. Maybe he did things you disapproved of, but we all do things our parents are not happy about." He put his hand on his heart. "My mother... she..." he shook his head and locked his eyes on Rick's with grim intensity. "I will help you avenge your son."

* * *

It was near midnight when they brought the man to him. His once expensive suit was torn, soiled and bloody.

"I have someone to see you, Mr. Jennelo." Boris slammed the man into the metal folding chair. The moon was bright and full, shining, with its slanting rays coming through the window at his back. The light gleamed on the man's slick backed hair highlighting the gray streaks in it that Rick Jennelo was sure the man considered distinguished. The man raised his head. His lips had been pulped, swollen and bloody from heavy punches to his face. Rick looked at the deep, fresh, cuts and the swelling of the knuckles on the hand's Boris had on each of the man's shoulders pinning him to the chair as he squirmed. The man stopped moving and looked at him.

"You must be Tyler's father." He spat a glob of blood filled with bits of broken teeth but it didn't get far. The slimy spittle hung from his chin and swayed with his deep breathing.

Rick glanced at Boris, who stepped away. "Yes." He moved closer and placed the muzzle of the .357 Magnum between Carlos's eyes and pulled the trigger. The back of his head exploded and that gray hair was no longer there to shine in the moonlight. He looked down at the slumping body in the fancy, now blood-drenched, suit. "I am Tyler's father."

Chapter 30

ITHACA, NEW YORK

Three days after talking with Mr. Jennelo, Ryan got home from work and found he had left a message with an address for Avery in Detroit. He would have to look at a city map to be sure but he thought the address was in the middle of the shitty part of town.

Two days after that he called him at The Wolverine to let him know he was on the road for the seven hour, 404-mile, drive from Ithaca, New York to Detroit. Every minute and every mile were filled with the feeling that he wasn't driving. He was sliding backward and down into a deep, dark, hole. One that he didn't know if he'd ever be able to climb back out of.

* * *

**JUNE 30, 1991
DOWNTOWN DETROIT**

Ryan walked past without recognizing the nondescript man on the bench. The man looked up at him and in an almost painful, low, voice whisper-sang. "I'm still on the front porch sittin' on my behind—waitin' for you."

The line from that song made Ryan stop and turn. "Avery?"

"Yeah, it's me." The man on the bench was a good 20 or 30 pounds lighter than the chiseled form of the friend Ryan had known. His once rich, mahogany colored, skin was now ashen gray.

"What are you doing here?"

"Can we talk?" Avery scanned around him. "Off the street?"

Ryan noticed the men on the corner and across the street watching them. "Sure. My car's right back there." Ryan pulled his keys out and turned to retrace his steps to where he had parked. He looked over his shoulder at Avery. The men on the other side of the road paralleled them. Ryan walked faster and Avery kept up with him.

"I heard you were looking for me. Why are you here? You need a change of view from the hallways of the Ivy League?" His laugh had a hint of pain and scorn in it.

Ryan unlocked the car and held the door for him. "Want to grab a beer? Let's find a bar..." He looked around. "A nice bar."

"Yeah. Sure." He looked at the litter of empty fast food wrappers and Styrofoam coffee cups inside the car. "Same car... same issues." He grinned and Ryan got a glimpse of his old friend inside the changed man in the seat next to him.

Ryan laughed and they rode in silence for ten minutes. He pulled into a bar parking lot and five minutes later two beers were in front of them. "So what's up with you?" He sat across from Avery and took a sip. "You don't look too good."

"Adult life has been harder than I thought."

Ryan took a bigger drink. "Don't I know that." He stretched his left leg out. His knee still ached. "I'm sorry about your grandmother. I would've come for her service but I was dealing with this." He rubbed his left knee. "I tried calling you and left a couple of messages on your machine. When I didn't hear back in a few days, I tried again and the phone number had been disconnected."

Avery nodded and looked at Ryan's outstretched leg. He'd heard how Ryan had never fully recovered from blowing his knee out. "I kept reinjuring my shoulder and so much shit was going on with grandma getting sick. After she had died, I screwed around and lost my scholarship. I was pretty messed up." He set the beer down untasted. "Ryan, I need some help."

"First, I have to tell you Tyler's dead."

"I heard. Mr. Jennelo called me to let me know. He mentioned you'd be in town today looking for me. I knew you'd drive straight through and worked out the timing." As bad as that news about Tyler was, he was not surprised. Tyler had gotten in with some very bad people. He had heard the talk on the street about the young man-boy that was working for Carlos that had tripled his street distribution. "I feel bad that things ended that way for him. But, I might end up the same way only in an alley here and not in Mexico."

Ryan looked at him. He had known him his entire life and Avery had never asked for his help. It must be a bad situation. "What kind of trouble are you in?"

Avery looked at him. All he could think of was that if he hadn't done what he did that night, then things would've turned out so much different for all of them. "I'm sorry Ryan. So sorry for what I did."

Ryan blinked. "Avery, it's done—and we were all responsible."

"That's not what I mean." Avery shook his head. "Not what I mean," he whispered. He looked up. "I need money. I'm into some very bad people that I owe. If I don't pay them, they'll kill me."

Ryan stood and drained his beer. "Let's talk about that on the road. We're headed to see Tyler's father at The Wolverine.

"I need to get something from my car. Can we swing by it so I can grab some stuff?"

* * *

"Do you remember homecoming parade our senior year?" Avery asked as they pulled into the small off-street parking area for The Wolverine.

Ryan rubbed his eyes with the back of his hand. "Yeah." He rotated his head and stretched his neck trying to work the stiffness out. He still hadn't shaken off the drive from Ithaca. "You remember the big plans they had for us once we won State? It was sure to be a long carnival parade." It came out and he bit his lip but couldn't take it back. He was tired and wasn't thinking who he had made that comment to.

"Yeah. I do." He didn't need to look over to see. He knew Avery had slumped further down in the seat. "I fucked that one up for everyone, didn't I?"

* * *

THE WOLVERINE

The bar had a few regulars in it but was mostly empty. The jukebox was still the same and they sat at the large back table nearest it. Ryan looked at Mr. Jennelo. "I remember coming down here to help Tyler clean up when the bar was closed and he'd feed that all day and sing along."

Mr. Jennelo's smile flashed for a second. "You know I can't sing. Never could hold a note. But Tyler's mother, she could sing beautifully." The smile was gone and the expression of a man that had lost the two loves of his life returned. "She didn't live too long after Tyler was born but somehow he got that love of music from her."

Avery, who had been quiet since they came in, laughed. "He sure didn't get her voice... man, he was awful." He shook his head. "But that didn't stop him from trying."

Rick Jennelo looked at them. From the day he'd stood on the sidelines when Tyler was 8 years old and began playing football for the Shelby Lions, and met the new friends he'd made... he had watched them grow into men. He turned to Avery. "Tell me what's going on, Avery. I hear a lot of talk about you and Carpenter Dave."

At first, Ryan thought his friend wasn't going to talk about it. His head had dropped and he looked down at the scarred and nicked surface of the table, not them. He reached over and gripped his shoulder and gave it a squeeze. Avery looked up and across the table at Mr. Jennelo.

"You know, Mr. Jennelo. You've bailed me out before. I can't ask you to do it again."

"Amanda called me when she heard about Tyler's death." Rick Jennelo waved at the bartender to bring him some more coffee. "We talked for a long time. I always thought she was a remarkable girl." He glanced at Ryan, who shifted in his chair. The bartender brought the coffee pot and poured into the empty cup next to him. "Thanks, Lou." He looked at the man who nodded and went back to the small kitchen in the back. He looked at Ryan for a moment and then Avery. "We talked about all of you. And, Avery..." he waited for Avery to make eye contact. "She said she had found a program that might be just the thing to help you get your life back on track." He took a slip of paper from his pocket with some information written on it. "Do you want to?"

"Want to what, sir?"

"Get things turned around. Get off the pills and booze... stop gambling your life away." He handed the note to Ryan. "If you'll work at it I think your friends will help you."

Ryan was tired of his oldest friends being part of a past he'd tried to forget and move beyond. "I'll help you, Avery." He raised the paper. "I'll stay in town a couple of days and we'll check this out."

"Avery?"

They watched as he took a deep breath and then sat straighter in his chair. "Yes, sir. I want to turn things around." He looked at Ryan. "I need help."

"In some ways, I let Tyler end up following the path he went down. I know he believed that I had left him no alternative. And..." he studied Avery, who met his look. "I'm responsible for what got you started down a different but equally bad path, too. I made a bad decision then but the thing about life is, boys..." He leaned back in his chair and caught each of their eyes then continued. "You can't erase a bad decision. All you can do is try to make good ones each day from that point on." He rose from the table and headed toward his office. "I'm going to call Carpenter Dave and get the slate wiped clean for you." He stopped and put a hand on Avery's shoulder. "You go with Ryan and get into this program, Avery. You're young enough to fix your life."

* * *

RAMADA INN
DETROIT

Ryan tossed the room key to Avery. "Room 207 is yours. I'm next to you in 209." They opened their doors at the same time and Ryan went in tossed his bag on his bed and opened the connecting door to their rooms. "I'm going to give Jacob's father a call." He saw Avery nod and head toward the bathroom.

He went over to the small desk and picked up the phone dialing for an outside line. "Mr. Winslow? This is Ryan Kramer." There was a pause and then Jacob's father answered reluctantly it seemed. "I know Jacob's not in yet but I'd like to leave a message for him. Yes. If you wouldn't mind taking it and giving to him. I'd appreciate it. I'm at the Ramada Inn and the number is 313-781-6254 room 209. Yes. If you would please give him that and ask him to give me a call or leave a message when he gets in. Thank you, sir--" Ryan looked at the phone in his hand. Mr. Winslow had just abruptly hung up on him.

He shook his head. Things had changed a lot after the investigation into Gavin's death. He had always thought that Mr. Winslow had suspected something and knew for certain that he had developed a dislike for Tyler and Avery. It looks like now he had lumped all of his son's old friends in the same category—the one's to keep away from Jacob.

Chapter 31

The priest's words were of little comfort. Ryan looked up from his shoes to Mr. Jennelo, who was standing right across from him. He knew that he was a hard man, a tough man, but always fair. No one else would have done what he had done for Avery. He didn't know what had gone wrong between him and Tyler, but regret stretched his pale face tight. Tyler was all the family that he had since his wife died.

Ryan rubbed his eyes and looked left and right at who was beside him. Jacob, tall and stiff in a gray suit, white shirt, and black tie was next to him. He would be leaving for the airport right after the funeral. He had to get back to USC and prepare for the upcoming season. The brief moments before the funeral weren't the right time, so he hadn't talked to him about what it was like to play on that stage—at a major college—with 80,000 cheering fans. Ryan had watched every game that he could to see one of his oldest and best friends, in the arena they had both loved, doing so well. It was like watching a god hurl thunderbolts that streaked across the emerald field. He rubbed his knee and felt its deep ache.

He looked at Tyler's casket and then across it at Avery standing next to Mr. Jennelo. It was too much death. For all of them to be so young and have people die around them on top of what had died inside them. Avery's spirit as it crashed and never rose from the field with that fumble at the end of the playoff game. Gavin at Torch Lake.

Tyler bitter and hell-bent on forging a dark future that he'd never contemplated but felt was all he had—and it had consumed his brash, brave, friend. Kelly's miscarriage that weighed so heavily on him. His own hopes and dreams as he clutched his ruined left knee, writhing in pain, on the field of his first college game; the only one he would ever play. And now Tyler, hopefully finally at peace, in front of him. Dead. All dead.

He felt her take his right hand and thought that too, had been dead—what he'd had with Amanda was special but no more. She had been standing next to him the whole time, as quiet as she always was, but there for him as she always had been. Except for those times when he'd been too stupid and too angry to stick with her. So much time wasted. He shook his head and lifted her hand to his lips. He lowered it and turned to look at her. "I'm sorry Amanda, so, so sorry." He felt the tears welling and starting to trickle down his cheek. There were so many things to cry for he didn't know which or who they were for... Maybe... Probably for all of them. Her hand came up and wiped them away.

"Shhhh... It's going to be okay, Ryan. It's all going to be okay." She smiled, albeit sadly, at him.

He looked across again at Avery, who was watching them. Avery seemed fragile. The suit, in a dusty, dirty garment bag, he'd pulled from the trunk of his car looked big on him and had been last worn at his grandmother's funeral. He, maybe more than any of them, had been through so much. The priest finished and they paid their last respects. Amanda placed a single rose on the casket as she filed by. Avery and Jacob each put a hand on the casket and bowed their head for a moment then moved away. Ryan stepped to the side of the casket and took out something that he hadn't worn since high school graduation. It was his class ring. On one side was a football player charging forward with the football tucked away. He, Tyler,

Jacob, and Avery each had the same design. Even though Ryan knew it was intended to be a tailback or a fullback, he knew Tyler had always envisioned his as him returning that interception for a touchdown to win the championship game in the closing seconds. On the opposite side of the ring was stamped the words VICTORY. Wearing that ring and being a champion had meant everything in the world to him. As it had for Tyler, Avery, and Jacob. They each had sworn to wear theirs until they could replace them with a championship ring. Avery had pawned his long ago. He rolled the ring in the palm of his hand then placed it on the casket and walked away. A championship, he shook his head. Now only Jacob would ever win and wear rings like that.

He saw that Amanda, Avery, and Jacob had waited for him near the cars. As he approached them, he saw the hesitant smile on Amanda's face again. He looked over his shoulder and saw the last person remaining at Tyler's graveside. It was his father. He stood there, head hanging down, beside his son's body.

"I've got to get back to LA but I'm hoping you guys can come out for a game this season. I can get you tickets and you can crash at my apartment." Jacob walked forward his hand out. "It was good to see you, Ryan. Really good. I'm sorry my dad didn't give me your message. But, I'll do a better job of keeping in touch with you guys." He smiled at Amanda and Avery. "Avery you get things straight, okay. That program Amanda found that Ryan's going with you to check out tomorrow, it sounds like it will help." He shook Avery's hand and clasped him on the shoulder. He turned and gave Amanda a hug then walked over to his dad's car. With a wave of his hand, he pulled away.

"And…" Amanda hitched her purse up on her shoulder. "I've got to get home and change for work. I wish I didn't have to go. I'd like to hang out with you guys more." She gave Avery a quick hug and turned to Ryan. "I know you've got things to take care of, too but maybe tomorrow before you head to Detroit to drop off Avery and then back to Ithaca... maybe, I'll see you?" She brushed a lock of hair back behind her ear and looked at him doubtfully.

Ryan stuck his hands in his pockets and felt like a 16-year-old teenager afraid to make eye contact and ask a girl out on a date. He had hurt her so much already and he didn't know if he had anything to offer her. He would probably be able to find a decent job when he got out of school but where it would be he didn't know. And would she even wait for him. "Yeah. I'll give you a call and maybe see you on the way out of town tomorrow." He looked up at her and nodded then asked, Avery. "You ready to go?"

They got in his car and he watched her drive away until she was down the road and out of sight. He cranked the engine and put it in gear. "Anything special you'd like to do tonight. You want to eat out or go to a club?" He glanced at Avery.

Avery coughed then grinned. "I think I'd rather just sit and eat pizza at the hotel and talk... It's been a long time since I've had anyone to just talk to. It's good to see you, man. I've really missed all of you."

* * *

RAMADA INN
ROOM 207
DETROIT

There was one slice of thin-crust pepperoni left in the two large pizza boxes they'd stopped and picked up along with a six pack of beer before they got back to the hotel. Other than chewing, drinking, and a belch or two they'd been quiet. Avery looked over at Ryan who was sitting with the chair turned so he could put his feet up on the bed. "I don't think you feel much like talking. At least to me." He reached over and slapped Ryan's feet off the bed and smiled. "But I think I know who you'd really like to be with right now." His grin broadened.

Ryan sat up. "I don't know if she wants that."

"I saw the way that she was looking at you earlier today. She still loves you. Hell, she's loved you since our sophomore year." Avery scratched his head and leaned back in his chair. "And I know that through all the bullshit you still love her." He reached over and grabbed Ryan's car keys sitting on the table between the pizza boxes. He tossed them and they landed in Ryan's lap. He looked at his watch. "I think she said she usually gets off in an hour."

Ryan sat up brushing pizza crumbs from his chest and wiping his mouth and chin with a napkin. He stood. "Okay, I'm gonna go talk to her when she gets off, for an hour or so. But I'll be back for us to hang out okay? I promise you." Avery laughed and it sounded kind of sad. Ryan turned back to him from the door. "Seriously, I know we need to talk. I'll be back."

* * *

SHELBY SENIOR LIVING CARE CENTER

Thirty minutes later Ryan pulled into the care center parking lot. He walked in and at the front desk counter were two older ladies. One was thin with a narrow, stern, face and had her hair pulled tightly back into a bun. The other was shorter, plump, with long, straight, hair framing the face of a smiling cherub. "Excuse me. If it's possible, I'd like to see Amanda for just a minute. It won't take long."

The two women eyeballed him and didn't say anything. After a pause, the thin one picked up a clipboard and looked at it. "She's in B-Wing right now but doesn't get off for another three hours."

"Three hours! I thought she got off at seven?" Ryan ran a hand through his hair and looked at the clock on the wall behind the two women.

The round-faced one stood and looked over the shoulder of the other woman. "No. It looks like when she came in, she decided to pick up some hours from Alice. She's not off until ten."

"Can I see her... just for a minute." Ryan looked around and saw the door to the right of the front desk area and behind the women with a large B on the front. He headed toward it.

"Young man, you can't go back there." The round woman was no longer smiling. She came from behind the desk and when he went through the door, she was right behind him yapping like one of those dogs you can't get to shut up. "Stop. Stop!"

Though she was in the very rear of the wing, the tile floor echoed every sound. Amanda heard the noise headed her way and wondered what was going on now. It seemed like every time she worked a double that spanned the night shift, Ms. Tharp the shift supervisor always watched her and complained about her work. She always wore tight pants and that might be the reason why she was so bitchy.

Amanda carefully wiped her face checking that it was with a clean cloth and not the one she'd been using to clean up Mr. Holloway's mess. Why his bladder and bowels would let go every time he left his room she didn't know. But they did. And now she smelled of the mess and would the rest of the night. She heard two sets of steps coming closer. They were just around the corner in the main passageway that led to and from the office. One of them was a flat, fast, stomping that she recognized and the other was a lighter, lengthier, stride. She mopped up the last of it and put the rag in the pail with the filthy, foul, water and stood. As she did Ryan came around the corner. He stopped and stared at her. Christ, she thought, I'm a mess and I stink.

He thought she was the most beautiful thing in the world. He didn't hesitate and strode forward lifting and cradling her in his arms. He tilted his head down to kiss her lips. He had dreamed thousands of times of doing that again. "I love you, Amanda. If you take me back, I'll never ever leave or hurt you again."

Behind him, Ms. Tharp's yelping had turned harsh. "Put her down! Amanda, you have to get back to work... and he should not be back here!"

Amanda didn't pay any attention to the woman but Ryan did and put her down. He kept ahold of her hand. "I love you Amanda and never want to leave you. Walk with me back to the front and then I'll wait there until you get off."

The surly supervisor followed them all the way back to the front entrance. When they were across from her father's room, Amanda saw him come out curious about the noise no doubt as other patients were. He looked at them. Ryan paused knowing that he was her father. She didn't think he'd recognize him or her and she was aware her ID badge wasn't positioned where he could read her name. He stepped forward and put his left hand on Ryan's shoulder as his right softly stroked Amanda's hair and then her cheek. She saw his eyes clear, something she had not seen in a very long time, and he smiled. He leaned in and gave her a kiss on the cheek. When he straightened, she saw his eyes were cloudy and confused again. He didn't say anything as he turned to go back into his room. He shut the door behind him.

Ryan continued to the B-Wing entrance door. He swung around to face her and let her hand go. "I'll wait for you." He went through it into the lobby and sat down and looked at Amanda, who stood there with the red-faced round woman scowling at them both. "I'll be right here when you get off." Behind the counter, the thin woman's tight face had cracked into a big smile.

* * *

RAMADA INN
ROOM 207

It was 8:10 PM and Ryan still hadn't returned. Avery looked at the empty beer cans on the table. But going out to get more beer didn't appeal to him. He opened the adjoining door into Ryan's room. He knew he'd find something better there and did. In the bathroom was a half-full fifth of Crown Royal and a water glass. He grabbed the bottle and glass and returned to his room where he sat it on the table and picked up the ice bucket. Sticking his room key in his pocket, he went down the hall filled the ice bucket and came back.

He looked at his watch 8:20 PM. He laughed to himself. So much for Ryan being serious. Then he felt bad immediately after thinking that. For as fucked up as his life had been, the others, except Jacob, had dealt with some shit as well. He wasn't the only one that had things to cry about. If things between him and Amanda could come together, she and Ryan deserved it.

He quickly drank two full water glasses with just a little ice. He looked at his watch again 8:35 PM. Right about now things would be jumping at the Russian's downtown casino. God how he wished he hadn't fucked things up so bad and could go back there. He sat there watching the ice cubes in the bottom of his glass melt and thought about that. He took out the sealed grease splattered envelope he had retrieved from the trunk of his Escort along with his suit and a baggie of necessities when he and Ryan had swung by his shit-hole apartment. He opened it and surprisingly they were still in there. He thought for sure during one of his blind drunk or drugged moments he would've tapped that or used it. And when sober, he'd always been afraid to check and see if it was still there. Because the thought of it not being there would truly mean that he had lost everything that his grandmother had worked so hard to give him.

His fingers touched the edges of strapped greenbacks. He remembered the night he'd won that first big roll of cash, $30,000, and in a moment of surprisingly forward thinking he had hidden part of it away. It was his last $10,000.

He had turned the radio on as he drank but left the volume low. He heard the iconic opening to one of his favorite oldies. He reached to turn it up and then sat back with the remnants of the fifth in his glass. As the last line rang in his head, 'tell me that you are not a thief... oh, but I'm bad company 'til the day I die,' he thought about Frank's place, the downtown casino, and then about Ryan and where he was. He knew—hoped—that maybe something good had happened with Amanda and they were together. He had decided that no matter what the program looked like tomorrow when he and Ryan went to check it out he was going to sign up, go through it and come out clean and sober. But, he stroked the bills and thought, I want one last shot at the tables and then I'll walk away clear of that, too. He swallowed the last of his drink.

* * *

CASINO – FRANK'S PLACE

DOWNTOWN DETROIT

Thirty minutes later he got out of the taxi a block from the casino and walked up. The big Russian, Boris, was at the door. He had seen him a few times at The Wolverine talking with Tyler's dad. Boris recognized him and held a hand out that was bigger than Avery's head to stop him from going inside. "Haven't you learned your lesson?"

"Not today my friend, I'm going to make a run. Call Frank and tell him I'll play with cash only. I have $10,000 on me."

Boris tilted his head and chin down to the left to the microphone on his lapel. Avery couldn't hear what was said but he looked up and nodded at him. "Show me the cash."

Avery slipped the band off and fanned the bills. Boris took them from him and checked them with a tiny, pocket, UV light and under a small magnifying glass. "Those look okay to you?"

Boris bent his head to the microphone again. Word came back into the earpiece he wore in his left ear and he nodded again and opened the door for Avery.

Frank met him just inside the door. "This wouldn't happen if Carpenter Dave was here right now. I like you, Avery. Always have. But let me see the money."

Avery handed him the bills and watched as Frank checked them as well. He handed them back and Avery put them in his pocket. "Okay, that's all you got. Make it last if you can." Frank walked over to the floor boss and whispered in his ear and then waved Avery over and gave him louder instructions. "The minute he's tapped out you have security show him the door."

* * *

With a nice crisp buzz building and the weight of his outstanding debt off his shoulders, Avery let the chimes of the slot machines bring a glow to his everyday sedated state. He felt a new beginning was ahead of him and good luck would follow. Kim, his favorite waitress, approached him with her ample breasts compressed into a one-size too small cocktail dress.

"It's nice to see you again. Would you like something to drink?"

"My favorite good luck charm is here!" He stroked her shoulder. "How about a double Absolut and cranberry."

Seconds later, drink in hand, Avery butted up to his old nemesis, the Blackjack table. He popped the gold 10-thousand-dollar band off the bundle as he slid the money to the dealer. "Let's do it." Two hands at $2,000 head to head with the dealer.

Kim dropped off another cocktail as Avery focused on the cards. He glanced at her. "Keep them coming." Quick losses left Avery with $4,000. To get back to a healthy stack of chips he pushed it all on one hand. The dealer's lightning hands snapped out a 19 to Avery and an up card of a King of Spades for the house.

Before Kim returned with his third drink, Avery waved off a hit and the dealer flipped over the down card of a 10 of Clubs. Dealer 20." As the dealer raked in his last stack of chips, Avery knew in his mind there was no way his life would reset to the one that was once so full of promise. There was no roller coaster chip counts or the thrill of a great double-down or Blackjack. Just a swift kick in the balls that had put him down so many times before. The search for a new beginning and that elusive rush was not to be found. His numb body felt just like the day he had left the field at their last playoff game. The day that had closed out his high school football career.

Done. Busted down to zero. Avery didn't know what to say and could barely look at Frank as he walked out.

"Avery. Hey, Avery!"

He turned around. It was Frank.

"Have you got cab fare to get you where you need to go?"

Avery couldn't even speak but shook his head.

For a moment, Frank looked much older and sadder. He walked over to Avery and took two $100 bills out of his pocket and put it in his hand. "Sorry, kid."

* * *

RAMADA INN
ROOM 207

Avery opened his hotel room door. It was dark inside. He had forgotten to leave a light on. It didn't matter. There wasn't much to see anyway. He knocked on Ryan's door but there wasn't any answer and he couldn't see any light through the opening at the bottom of the door above the carpet. He sat down and realized that he would always be fucked up. He could sit and think of reasons why he had just done what he had done. But it made no sense.

He had told Ryan, Jacob and Amanda that he was ready to put all this shit behind him. Losing that stupid fucking football game. Losing a scholarship to play at a low-level community college. The gambling, all the chips that had slipped through his fingers, and losing the money his grandmother had given him that had taken her decades of hard work to save. He had let Mr. Jennelo down, too; maybe him most of all. He shook his head, disgusted with himself.

He sat on the floor next to his bed and watched the LED indicator on the hotel room clock change minute by minute. He reached into the bag he had carried in and brought out the two fifths of Crown Royal he had made the cabbie stop to pick up from a liquor store. He filled the water glass to the brim. From his front pocket, he took out the baggie with the last of his pills. He had thought about throwing it out a dozen times to remove the temptation. Now he was glad that he hadn't. There was enough left to take the edge off of his latest failure.

Chapter 32

RAMADA INN
ROOM 209

Ryan felt bad as he parked his car that morning and hurried into the hotel. He had promised Avery that he'd be back but hadn't expected what had happened with Amanda and sure hadn't expected to spend the night with her. He had tried calling his hotel room last night at 9:00 and as soon as Amanda got off to let him know but hadn't got an answer. In his room, on his way to take a quick shower and change, he knocked on the connecting door putting his mouth close to it, "Avery—Avery! It's Ryan. I'm sorry about last night, man. I was with Amanda. I'm gonna take a quick shower and then I'll tell you about it." He didn't wait to listen for a reply and grabbed his shaving kit and headed to the bathroom.

Ten minutes later, skin still red from the hot shower, with a towel wrapped around him he knocked on the connecting door again. "Hey, man. It's time to get up and get going I got a lot to talk to you about." There wasn't any answer. He put his ear to the door and couldn't hear anything coming from the other room. He tried the knob and the door was locked. He walked over to the phone on the small desk in the corner and dialed Avery's room number. He could hear ringing both in the earpiece and through the wall. No answer. He pulled his pants on and yanked a t-shirt over his head. Remembering to stick his room key in his pocket he stepped into the hallway. He knocked on the door to Avery's room and waited. After a minute, he knocked again. There still wasn't any answer and he couldn't hear any movement in the room. He heard someone coming down the hallway and looked to his right. It was a maid trundling a cart full of towels and housekeeping supplies.

"Excuse me. Have you seen anyone go in or out of this room this morning?"

The woman shook her head. "No, but it's on my list to clean." She looked down at his bare feet and then up at his face. "Is there something wrong, sir?"

Ryan shook his head. "I don't know. I'm in the room next to this one." Ryan pointed at his hotel room door. "This is the room I booked for my friend—we're together, I mean traveling together—and he should be in there. But he's not answering."

The maid looked at the doorknob and then at the clipboard on her cart. "There's not a Do Not Disturb sign on the knob and I don't see any notes that the occupant had asked for late checkout or that they've already checked out. Maybe he just went out for breakfast." She seemed impatient to get on with her work.

"No, he would not have gone out without letting me know or leaving a message. Can you open the door for me?"

"I can't do that sir. Only the manager, Mr. Jensen, can authorize that."

Ryan stepped away from Avery's door and over to his. "Please, I'm going to step into my room and call the front desk and speak with the manager. Will you wait here and then you can confirm it with them."

The woman sighed and shrugged her shoulders. "I'll work in the room right across then," she gestured at a door opposite his. "You let me know when you're done talking with them and then I'll check that Mr. Jensen says it's okay."

"Thanks." Ryan nodded and opened his door stepping inside. At the desk phone, he dialed zero. "Hi, this is Ryan Kramer in room 209. If you check my account and registration, I also booked room 207. Right. My friend Avery Irons has that room but he's not answering the phone or the door and I'm worried that something might've happened to him. Yes, I understand... I understand that. But you can confirm that I'm the person that made the reservation, checked in and paid for both rooms, right? Mr. Irons has some health problems and I'm worried that something might be wrong. If you want, you can have your security guard come up and enter the room. I just want to make sure that my friend is okay. Can you do that? Great, thank you. I'll watch for the guard."

Ryan opened his door and stepped across the hall and knocked on the slightly open room door where the housekeeper was working. "Ma'am," he pushed the door open a bit further and slid past the cart. "Ma'am, the manager is sending up a security guard to check room 207."

She looked up from straightening the comforter on the king-size bed and nodded. Finishing she followed him out into the hall. In about a minute Ryan saw a blue uniformed gray-haired man coming down the hall taking a big ring of keys from the clip on his belt. He nodded at the maid. "Maggie, is there a problem with 207?" She shrugged and pointed at Ryan.

"I don't know if there's a problem or not but I'm worried about my friend. I appreciate you going in and checking to see if he's in there." Ryan stepped away from the door to give the guard room.

The guard had selected a key but didn't insert it in the knob. He rapped lightly on the door and looked at Ryan. "What's his name?"

"It's Avery. Avery Irons. I tried calling and knocking but there's no answer."

"And you're sure he's just not off somewhere getting breakfast?"

Ryan shook his head. "No. He wouldn't do that without leaving me a message."

The guard nodded. "Okay." He knocked louder on the door. "Mr. Irons, this is hotel security. Please open the door." He waited a minute and when there wasn't a response, he knocked again. "Mr. Irons, this is hotel security and I'm opening the door and entering the room." He inserted the key and turned it. Pushing the door open it caught on the security latch. "Someone's in here." He took a tool from his belt and inserted it, jimmying it up, to release the security latch. He opened the door wide and held it there with the flat of his left hand and called again. "Mr. Irons, this is hotel security and I'm coming in this room." He started to enter the room and Ryan was right behind him. He stopped and looked over his shoulder. "You stay here in the hallway." He entered and the door started to close. Ryan stepped forward and stuck his foot in to keep it from shutting. Then he heard the guard's sharp breath from inside the room and distinct mutter. "Shit!" Ryan swung the door wider and went in.

The room was messy. He saw the guard's shoulders and head above the other side of the bed. He came further into the room and looked at what the guard was kneeling next to. It was Avery. His eyes had rolled back in his head, his mouth was slightly open and dried bile trailed from a corner of his mouth down his chin. The guard had placed two fingers at Avery's throat to check for a pulse. He looked up at Ryan and shook his head.

Ryan staggered back. He barely heard the security guard, now on his radio. "Desk—we got a situation. The man in 207 is dead. Right. I'm sure. Call 911 and get EMTs and the police here. I'm going to secure the room."

Ryan looked at the scrap of a newspaper that sat on the small table next to two bottles of Crown Royal, one empty and one three-quarter empty. The glass beside it had held ice—now melted – the condensation ring spreading from its bottom to seep onto a scrap of newsprint making it translucent. A car ad bled through from the other side. It, for the most part, had been carefully torn from the newspaper. The top left corner had a ragged rip through it taking out most of the headline and beginning:

> "...was once one of Metro Detroit's best athletes playing
> on Utica Eisenhower's first undefeated, regular season,
> football team in 1988. Services will be held July 1, 1991,
> at St. Johns Cemetery, Shelby Township."

He shook his head. So much had been lost... all because of a game. He felt someone at his side. The guard had risen from the body and approached him.

"Sir... Sir, you need to go back to your room and stay there. The police are on their way and they're going to have questions for you."

Ryan left the room and stepped around the wide-eyed maid, unlocked and entered his room. He sat down on the end of his bed with his head in his hands. *Jesus fucking Christ, another friend I could've helped... that I should've helped sooner, is dead.*

* * *

FALL 1991
THE WOLVERINE
DETROIT

"That Winslow kid, at USC, he's tearing it up isn't he, boss?" Lou had worked for Rick Jennelo for more than 20 years. He had the pulse of everything that went on in and around The Wolverine.

"What's that, Lou?" Rick Jennelo looked up from the sheets of paper spread on his desk.

"That kid, the QB at USC, the one who was friends with…" Lou swallowed what he was about to say. His boss hadn't mentioned his son's name since the funeral service. For a while, he had been even quieter than he usually was but his mood seemed to have lightened lately. He wondered why since during that time he had also been paying out bets weekly for months, mostly small, on USC football. He started again. "I mean USC keeps covering the spread."

Jennelo shrugged and studied the paper in front of him. "He's a helluva quarterback."

Lou didn't get it; he knew that even losses on small bets added up over time. "Why is there so much, small-money, local traffic? Why'd you decide to handle those?"

Rick Jennelo stood and came around the desk closer to Lou. "Tyler was friends with Jacob Winslow since they were 8 years old. I watched those boys, Tyler, Jacob, Avery and Ryan grow up. They all had physical gifts and talent. Unfortunately, only one of them is still able to enjoy it on the field. Jacob."

"That Ryan Kramer kid, he blew his knee out right?" Lou had not heard his boss talk about those boys like this since they had graduated. He couldn't tell if that was a good thing or not.

"Right. He'll never play again and Avery and my son are dead..." he paused. "I've seen people with potential in life die young. People I love. And I wonder what my life would be like if they had lived. If my son had made different choices. If I'd been a better father to help him to learn to make better choices. It's the same thing with Avery when he needed a father-figure to give him better advice. I let them down and so I wonder what life would be if things were different and they were alive. Ryan's turned into a good young man. He's doing well in school and will likely graduate early with honors. He's already getting job offers—good ones—and I'm proud of him. Jacob's a winner on the field and he's got everyone in Shelby following him. They..." he returned to his desk. "We want him to keep winning. All the way into the NFL."

Lou had not heard him say this many words, at one time, in months. Then his boss did something else he hadn't done in even longer. He smiled.

"Covering those bets when USC wins," he gestured at the sheets in front of him, "is a pleasure. It makes me happy that Jacob's having such success."

Chapter 33

**SPRING 1992
LAKE ST. CLAIR
DETROIT, MICHIGAN**

The boat rocked gently. Its stern was swinging slowly around the forward anchor chain moved by the wind that had kicked up. The sky close to the horizon had that orange sherbet color melting into the water. Ryan reached for the bottle of Crown Royal and filled two glasses. He handed one to Jacob and leaned back on the settee to drink half his in a swallow. He watched his friend and realized the significance of that he still saw him that way. Jacob was his friend again, through all the changes and all the strangeness of what had happened to them all since autumn of their senior year of high school. The music mixtape came to a song that pierced him: *Champagne Supernova* by Oasis.

Tyler was gone; they'd never hear his voice again. They would never hear him tell his stories of improbable encounters that always seemed to happen when they were not around. Never hear his bitching about messing with his Trans Am. Wouldn't see his stamina... being the last man standing when the final drink hit the table to end a long night of partying. Or hear him singing his favorite songs. The song, still playing, was one of them. They'd all liked it and Tyler would sing it, poorly, but with passion. Ryan sang softly. "Someday you'll find me... caught beneath the landslide."

"He loved that song." Jacob had leaned forward, forearms on his knees, cupping the still full glass in his hands.

"Yeah." Ryan shifted and sat up. "But man, he could not sing. As we drifted apart sometimes when we spoke on the phone, he'd close with singing, 'where were you while we were getting high.' I could sense he missed having a close friendship but didn't know how to say it... or try to mend fences."

They sat silently and each knew what they would miss most about him. They would never have to deal with his coarse but genuine nature and they should have appreciated it more when he was alive. Tyler was who he was, and you didn't ever have to question that. The boat creaked and they could hear and feel the wind as it moved over the water, over them and the boat and off into the trees onshore.

"All Avery wanted to do was run. Carry that ball." Ryan looked at Jacob, who nodded. "I sometimes wonder if he ever gave any thought beyond high school other than playing ball. I guess we all had that lost feeling at first when we graduated, but Avery couldn't move on from the past." He stretched his left leg and rubbed the knee. "Do you ever wonder what our lives would be like if he hadn't coughed up that damn ball?"

"All the time." Jacob shifted and looked around them. The wind had dropped. "I know in my heart he would still be alive."

Ryan nodded. "That game scarred us all, but that fumble crushed Avery's soul."

"He told me once that on the field, the ball in his hands, was the only time he felt in control and free." Jacob took a bigger gulp of his drink. "He just wanted to run." He shook his head. "And that last, most important carry of his life ended with something that haunted him. But even after that and though we all moved in different directions, I always thought we would just pick right up where we left off when enough time had passed." He drank again. "Dreams die..."

Ryan looked at Jacob, who seemed uncomfortable at what he had just said. Jacob's dream hadn't. In this, his junior year, he had finished the football season a Heisman Trophy candidate and had declared for the NFL draft. He was going to get a shot to play professional football at its highest level. Ryan turned to look at something in the water that wasn't there. He finished his drink. "And their bodies seem to hang around... it's hard to bury them and walk away." He put the empty glass between his feet. "You know when we all talked about what our life would be after college." He glanced at Jacob, who was looking out over the water, away from him. "It didn't turn out that way for me and I never thought it would include losing two of my closest friends. I thought the four of us would stay connected for life."

Jacob had turned back to him. "I can't apologize."

Ryan looked back to him. "What?"

Jacob took a swallow from his glass. "I can't be sorry for making it to where I am. You know, so close to doing what we all dreamed of." He had that mixed look of resolve and remorse. A conflicted coexistence of emotions when you have to deal with things as they are and not as you wish them to be or as they might have been.

"God how we looked forward to that summer after our senior year." Ryan stared into his empty glass; at its circular, semi-reflective bottom with that last bit of liquid that collected there. But that's a place where there aren't any answers. "It went bad so fast." He shook his head. "And now here we are."

"It looks like you and Amanda might make it." Jacob took another sip. "You know... be together."

"Yeah." Ryan's voice seemed uncertain.

"Hey." Jacob tapped Ryan on the knee to get him to look up. "You've loved her and she's loved you for years." He sat back and his eyes came up to meet his. "All that shit—all that happened—we can't change. You have something special with her. Use that to move forward. When it happened, I thought my dream was done. And that was all I had—football—and if it was lost, I was lost. But you've always been smarter than any of us. I know you had plans far beyond playing a game. Focus on that. Focus on what you still have, or can have, that's good and whole."

Ryan whisper-sang, "A dreamer dreams, she never dies..." He put the glass down and looked at Jacob. "She always believed in me didn't she?"

Jacob nodded. "Always."

"Then I can't let her down."

Jacob smiled. "No, you can't," and slapped Ryan on the shoulder.

They each sank back in their chairs, relaxing for the first time since they had stepped on the boat. It felt like a load had lifted from each of them by saying the things they had held inside unsaid for so long. Moments passed peacefully in that comfortable silence that only the closest of friends can accept—no need to talk more—just enjoying the other's company.

Ryan shifted. He'd thought of something Avery had said when he had met him on his return for Tyler's funeral. The devil's come to collect from us. "He got Tyler and then Avery. Do you think he'll come for us?" He gripped his bad knee hoping that it, the knee was all that he would have to pay with or sacrifice.

Jacob turned to him. "What?"

"Before Tyler's funeral, Avery told me he thought that the devil had come to collect because of what we did at Torch Lake?" Ryan bent his left leg and straightened it. "Do you think enough has been paid?"

Jacob's face paled under his tan. "I don't know."

Chapter 34

**SEPTEMBER 1993
CRITTENTON HOSPITAL
ROCHESTER, MICHIGAN**

All through her labor, he fretted with a mixture of anticipation and anxiety. Ever since they had found out they were expecting their first child, he knew that he was faced with something that no parent wants to have to do. Hiding something from their child. And it wasn't something innocuous or embarrassing. It wasn't something like an addiction, alcoholism or some other vice that would be difficult to deal with if it came out. What he had to hide was something much darker; much more damaging. It was something even his beautiful wife did not know.

She looked up at him, the man she loved at first sight in 10th grade, that she thought she had lost. So much had changed for him in just a few years. The loss of that high school playoff game was small compared to wrecking his knee and never being able to play the sport he loved again. Or the loss of two of his best friends. She saw the lines in his face. Too many for someone so young and she wondered again what it was that he kept from her. Since the nearly back to back funerals of his closest friends he had never talked about football. He didn't even care to watch it on television anymore. Their baby, their son, wriggled in her arms and she shifted her attention to him opening her hospital gown so that he could nurse.

Their parents had just left and it had been a noisy time of posing for photographs and their coos of love and admiration as each held their first grandchild. Now it was quiet with the only sound a suckling baby. Lying there the weight of her newborn son on her chest, she had never. been more content in her life. Her son was almost finished and she knew he'd soon be asleep. She watched her husband and caught that odd look of pride and worry that was so frequently on his face.

"Tyler, would you like your daddy to hold you?" Amanda lifted him up to Ryan.

He held him and felt a full measure of love; one that was certain and sure. But he knew he would have to raise his son and any other children while praying that no one ever found out what happened that night at Torch Lake. He looked down at his child. "I won't ever let you down, Tyler. I swear that I won't."

IKE'S
GYM

www.ingramcontent.com/pod-product-compliance
Lightning Source LLC
Chambersburg PA
CBHW031245120726
47905CB00002B/724